MY BIG FAT ZOMBIE GOLDFISH

FINS OF FURY

MY BIG FAT ZOMBIE GOLDFISH

GOLDFISH

FINS OF FURY

MO O'HARA

ILLUSTRATED BY MAREK JAGUCKI

FEIWEL AND FRIENDS

NEW YORK

A Feiwel and Friends Book
An Imprint of Macmillan

A CIP catalogue record for this book is available from the British Library

ISBN: 978-1-250-02921-8 (hardcover) / ebook (978-1-250-07688-5)

Feiwel and Friends logo designed by Filomena Tuosto

Originally published in the UK by Macmillan Children's Books,
a division of Macmillan Publishers Limited.

First published in the United States by Feiwel and Friends,
an imprint of Macmillan.

First U.S. Edition: 2015

10 9 8 7 6 5 4 3 2

mackids.com

To my husband, Guy

FRANKIE GOES WILD

CHAPTER 1

THE NOT-SO-GREAT OUTDOORS

It was sunset and the sky was zombie goldfish orange. I flipped open the lid of the water canteen hanging around my neck and whispered, "Look, Frankie, it's your color."

Frankie, my pet zombie goldfish, peered out of the canteen and snatched a quick peek at the sky. Then he swished his tail and went back to swimming in tiny circles. He was not impressed.

The next thing I knew, I face-planted into the mud on the trail as I tripped over my stupidly long bootlaces for about the fifth time today. I wasn't impressed with this "weekend trip" either.

"I think I've changed my mind about wanting

to go camping," I huffed as I wiped the mud off my chin.

Frankie thrashed a fin as if he was saying, "Yeah, right, sure. *Now* you tell me." When did Frankie learn how to be sarcastic in fin sign language?

"Cheer up, Tom," Pradeep said as he held out his hand to pull me back up. "It's gonna be the best weekend ever. I can't believe you nearly didn't come!"

"Yeah . . ." I began, snapping shut the lid of the canteen. I thought about how I'd tried to back out of the trip, but Mom said that I needed some fresh air so I was going and that was that. Then I looked at Pradeep's super-excited face. "It'll be great," I said, and forced out a smile.

"I'm still not really sure why you brought Frankie though," Pradeep whispered.

"I had to." I sighed. "Mom said that she was

going to do a mega spring clean. What if Frankie thought the Hoover was trying to attack him again and went all zombie-thrash-fish in front of Mom? I couldn't risk it!"

"Listen up, campers!" the group leader shouted. "There's a fork in the path ahead. Can anyone use their wilderness skills to work out which way to head?"

"Past the knife and spoon," I yelled, and giggled at my own joke.

No one else laughed. If there was tumbleweed in the woods, it would have blown past me at that exact moment.

Then Pradeep spoke up. "Wind blowing westerly. And it's blowing the campfire smoke toward us, so the camp must be due west."

"Good work, camper," the leader shouted back. "Let's get moving then."

Pradeep took his camping very seriously and he was good at it. He'd been camping with the Cubs lots of times. He knew how to read a map and use a compass. He could make a tent out of a sheet and a couple of sticks, and it would stay up all night too!

"I told you this camping trip was going to be epic!" said Pradeep, as we started walking again. "Meeting Sam Savage from *Savage Safari* AND Grizzly Cook! It's going to be BRILLIANT!"

I had just started to feel the beginnings of a corner of a real smile creep across my face when all the wind was knocked out of me as I was hoisted up by my backpack and dangled above the grass.

CHAPTER 2
HAPPY ZOMBIE TRAILS

"Right, morons," said Mark, my Evil Scientist big brother, as he grabbed me and Pradeep and pulled us out of earshot of the other kids. "This weekend, I don't know you and you don't know me." He glared at us. "You look at me, you talk to me, you even say my name, and I will pound you into the ground so far that they'll need a digger to get you out? Got it?"

"Got it!" Pradeep and I gulped at the same time. Mark let go of our backpacks and our feet sank back into the mud. Then he strode off toward the front of the line.

At that moment, my canteen flung itself over

my neck and started bouncing around on the ground. Frankie must have heard Mark's voice and gone all zombie mega-thrash fish. Frankie has held a grudge against Mark ever since he tried to murder him with his Evil Scientist toxic gunk and then flush him. Luckily Pradeep and I shocked Frankie back to life with a battery, and he's been our zombified fishy friend ever since.

I walked over and picked up the furiously bouncing canteen. "It's OK, Mark's gone now, Frankie," I whispered, popping open the lid.

"Hey, that kid who keeps falling over at the back of the line is talking to his water canteen again," one of the other campers shouted.

"Maybe he's just talking to the 'medical alert' kid," another kid suggested, laughing.

"It's not like anyone else would talk to them," I heard Mark yell as he strode to the front of the line.

Pradeep looked down at his trekking boots.

See, when all the moms and dads were saying

good-bye in the car park a couple of miles
back, they were *all* pretty embarrassing . . . but
Pradeep's mom probably managed to break the
Most Embarrassing Parent EVER world record.
First she kissed Pradeep on the head and hugged
him until his eyes almost popped out, right
in front of all the other
campers. Then she
looped a huge plastic
wallet with his
permission
slips, emergency
contact numbers
and huge
medicines list
around his neck.
He looked like one
of those kids being
shipped off on a
train somewhere in
World War II!

Worst of all, she practically yelled, "Right, my little soldier, I have packed the motion-sickness tablets and the sick bags, the diarrhea medicine (as you know how campfire cooking gives you a funny tummy), the insect repellent, the sunscreen, the bee-sting lotion, the hay-fever pills, the calamine lotion and twelve extra pairs of socks. You can never have too many clean pairs of socks."

Pradeep of course whipped off the plastic wallet as soon as his mom was out of sight. But it was too late. Everyone had seen it.

I slung Frankie's canteen back around my neck and pulled a squashed peanut-butter sandwich from my pocket. I took a bite and passed Pradeep the rest. "Mmmo mkeep mmoo mgooooming," I mumbled through my peanut-butter-filled mouth.

"To keep me going? Thanks," Pradeep said, easily translating my peanut-butter mumble.

That little energy boost gave Pradeep what my

BOING!

gran would call a spring in his step. His feet easily found the places in the path without stones or roots sticking up. He didn't even have to look down. I trudged along and tried to put my sneakers in his footprints so I didn't fall over *again*.

That was when the mosquito got me right on the neck. I turned and swatted it with my hand, and immediately banged into Pradeep, who I hadn't noticed had stopped dead in his tracks.

"Sorry!" I began. "I was just squashing a pterodactyl-sized mosquito that chomped me—"

"Shhhhhh," he whispered.

The other campers were a good twenty paces ahead of us now.

Then I heard a rustling off to our left.

"What was that?" Pradeep said.

CHAPTER 3

A GRIZZLY WAY TO START A TRIP

I turned toward the sound.

Frankie's eyes started to glow bright green as he peered out of the top of the canteen. His zombie fish senses must have told him something wasn't right.

Then we heard the rustling again. It was closer this time.

Pradeep and I both instantly shot each other a look that said, "Whatever it is, I don't want to find out right now!"

I got a spring in my own step after that, for sure. Drops of water sloshed from Frankie's canteen as we ran to catch up with the other campers. Night was falling and we could make out the glow of the campfire through the trees.

Just then we heard a far-off rumble. The wind picked up and the trees around us started to sway as the noise got louder and louder.

Pradeep gave me a look that said, "Does that sound like . . ."

"A helicopter?" I finished out loud.

A huge chopper flew into view, one of those military ones that drop soldiers into combat zones. As the blades thundered above our heads, Frankie started going nuts in the canteen. He popped his head out of the top, clearly ready for a fight. We stood there with the other campers, mouths hanging open, goldfish-style, while the door of the hovering helicopter opened and a man leaned out. Then he climbed out onto one of the skids at the bottom, hooked a rope over the rail, threw it out and started to climb down. No harness, no anything!

"It's Grizzly Cook!" cried Pradeep.

Grizzly slid down the rope and then leaped the last couple of yards to the ground. "Welcome, campers!" he shouted over the roar of the blades. "Your adventure starts now!"

Then he shook the rope and it fell away from the helicopter and tumbled to the ground. He waved the pilot off with a casual salute and everyone burst into applause.

"That guy really knows how to make an entrance," I said.

Pradeep didn't move. He was stunned into silence, which doesn't happen to Pradeep very often.

"Come on," I said. "We have to set the tent up and get Frankie out of this canteen and into something bigger so he can stretch his fins. Then I'll find him something green to nibble on for dinner."

Being a zombie goldfish and all, Frankie was really fond of green food. The mouldier the better really, but we'd have to see what we could come up with, out here in the wild.

Pradeep switched back into survival mode and he had the tent up and our sleeping bags inside in minutes. We got out our flashlights and went off into the area around the clearing to see what we could find for Frankie to eat.

"Where are you off to, mates?" Grizzly bounded out of the shadow toward us. I quickly put the lid

back on the canteen so he wouldn't see Frankie inside.

"We just thought we'd have a look around," I said.

"Ummm," Pradeep said. His awestruck brain freeze clearly hadn't worn off yet.

"You can't wander off on your own after nightfall, guppies," Grizzly said. "First rule of survival in the wild: 'Respect your surroundings and they will respect *you*.'"

"Can't we . . . *respectfully* wander off for a bit?" I asked.

"Not really, mate," he said with a laugh, "but nice try."

Pradeep snapped out of his daze. "Can we help gather water to put out the campfire later?" he asked.

"Rule fourteen of survival in the wild: 'Fire can save your life if you're safe with fire,'" recited Pradeep and Grizzly at the same time.

"All right, mate, good plan." Grizzly patted

Pradeep on the back. "There's a stream above the sheep line just a few minutes that way. Take your flashlights and these containers and I'll keep watch from here. But be quick!"

"What's a 'sheep line'?" I asked Pradeep as we walked off toward the stream to get the water.

"It's a point above where sheep graze. You can tell because there are no droppings. That means that the sheep won't have peed or pooed in the water so it's safe to drink," he said.

"Yuck! Too much information!" I groaned.

When we reached the stream Pradeep held
the flashlight while I filled up the first container
and tipped Frankie inside along with some
green slime I found in a nearby puddle. He was
really happy to stretch his fins and finally have
something to eat.

Looking at Frankie chowing down on the
green goo reminded me I was hungry too. I dug
through the pockets of my hiking jacket.

"Score! Another sandwich!" I said, holding out
a squished mess of bread and peanut butter.

That's when we heard a twig snap a couple of
yards away.

CHAPTER 4

BEWARE THE EYES OF THE MARSH

Pradeep turned instantly and shone his flashlight in the direction of the sound, and for a split second I thought I saw a pair of large yellow eyes.

I screamed, picked up the container with Frankie inside and bolted back toward the camp as fast as my legs could carry me.

Pradeep was right behind me, yelling, "Tom, wait for meeeee!"

Grizzly was there in a flash as we hit the clearing.

"I thought I heard a girl scream out there?" Grizzly cried. "Was she with you guys?"

The other campers looked on as I explained.

"Um . . . no, that might have been me. I mean, sometimes my voice gets a little high when . . ."

They started to giggle.

Grizzly jumped in. "You should have heard me when I was surprised by a leopard seal in the Antarctic. I thought my scream would shatter the iceberg I was standing on!" He smiled. "So did something spook ya in the dark out there?"

"Eyes!" Pradeep and I said at exactly the same time. "Yellow eyes!"

"There aren't any dangerous animals in Burdock Woods, but any critter's eyes can look spooky reflecting light at night. I'll check it out, just in case, eh?"

Grizzly trotted off in the direction of the stream while Pradeep and I took Frankie and the container of water over to the campfire.

When we sat down, some of the kids hanging out with Mark started making little "Eeek, a mouse!," "Argh, a spider!" fake screams.

"Let's sit somewhere else," muttered Pradeep,

so we got up and went over to the other side of the fire to collect some sticks and start cooking our hot dogs.

Grizzly came back a moment later with the other water container filled to the brim and set it down next to the one with Frankie in it. "Nothing up there but a couple of fidgety rabbits," he said with a grin.

The smells of smoky blackened hot dogs and sticky marshmallow goo mixed in the air. When we had stuffed ourselves, the campfire stories began.

Grizzly told us about some of the amazing adventures he'd had. It was a lot of jumping off things, swimming through things, climbing up things and eating bugs really, but Pradeep was hooked on every word.

"What about the Beast of Burdock Woods?" one of the campers piped up.

"Oh, that story's a load of garbage," Grizzly replied. "No one's ever proved that there is a 'beast' in these woods. It's a myth, a legend. I might as well go looking for a unicorn around here." Everyone laughed.

Then Mark spoke up. "I heard that some of the local farmers said that *something* killed a sheep. And that they keep hearing weird noises at night . . ."

"Well, young man, if you hear weird noises at night tonight, I'll tell you what they'll be . . ." Grizzly paused. "Me snoring! Apparently I growl like an African hyena in my sleep, or so says the missus!"

Everyone laughed again, except me and Pradeep.

"Are you sure there's nothing dangerous out there?" I asked.

"I tell you what," Grizzly said. "We've got the world's best safari tracker, Sam Savage, coming in tomorrow. If there's something dangerous out there, we'll find it! Although I'm sure *all* we'll find is rabbits, hares, maybe some roe deer and the like. Not a 'beast' in sight!"

He got up and stretched like an actual grizzly bear. "Now it's time for some shut-eye." He and the other group leaders started to kick dirt into the fire to bring it down.

"Let's get Frankie back in his canteen," I whispered to Pradeep. But before either of us could move, Grizzly strode over to where we were sitting, picked up a water container and flung the water toward the dampening flames.

"Nooooooooooooo!" I shouted, leaping up.

CHAPTER 5
CAMPFIRE FISH!

The fire made a fizzing sound as the water hit the flames.

"Are you all right, mate?" asked Grizzly. "You look like you've lost your best friend."

My eyes darted around looking for flashes of zombie goldfish orange in the smoldering charcoal and wood. "Frankie!" I gasped.

Then Pradeep grabbed my shoulder. He was carrying the other water container. A small orange head peeked out and a green bulging eye winked at me.

"Frankie . . . phew!" I sighed.

"What's that, mate?" Grizzly asked as some of

the other campers looked on and giggled.

"I mean . . ." I stalled, "um . . . *frankly* . . . you . . . umm . . . really ought to really make sure that the fire is out properly. Right?"

"Good plan, mate," Grizzly said, and motioned to Pradeep, who was still holding the other container. "Best give the fire another drink then."

Pradeep looked down at Frankie and back up at me. I had to think fast. I reached down and picked up the container. "Just grabbing a drink first," I said, and gulped Frankie into my mouth with one glug. Then I passed the container to Pradeep, who threw the rest of the water onto the dying embers of the campfire.

I could feel Frankie wriggling in my mouth as I tried to walk as fast as I could back to the tent. But Mark had other ideas. He sprang out from behind some bushes. "So, you and Pradeep seem to be making friends with Grizzly." He stood in front of me and blocked my way. "You two better not say anything to him about knowing me, or else."

I shook my head: no.

"Have you got that, moron?" He leaned into my face.

I nodded my head: yes this time.

I could feel Frankie throwing himself at my cheeks, desperate to get out of my mouth and get Mark!

Mark glared at my firmly closed mouth. My cheeks must have looked like a soccer ball was hitting the back of a net every time Frankie jumped around in there.

Grizzly walked up. "All right, mates, time to turn in for the night." He looked down at me and then back at Mark, who was now smiling in the creepy way that he can smile when he wants to look innocent.

"Everything OK?" Grizzly asked me. I nodded.

"You can tell me, mate." He paused. "Just spit it out."

I looked at Mark, then at Grizzly. Frankie threw himself at the back of my mouth and made me retch just as Pradeep ran up with one of his sick bags half-filled with water.

I turned and spat Frankie into the sick bag and quickly rolled up the top so no one could see what was inside.

"I think my hot dog went down the wrong way," I said to Grizzly.

Pradeep grabbed the bag off me and headed for our tent. "I'll throw that away for you," he said. I could see the bag shaking with what must have been a really angry Frankie inside as Pradeep walked away.

"Hope that's all it was," Grizzly said, looking from me to Mark. "Now get some sleep. Early start, and as I always say, rule seventy-eight of survival in the wild is: 'Rise with the sun and you'll be ready for fun.'"

I brushed my teeth about twenty times when we got back to the tent. Then Pradeep and I crawled into our sleeping bags and I found Frankie some green gummy bears to chew on as a treat. I ran my tongue across the inside of my mouth. "Bleugh, still gross!" The taste of slightly minty-flavored zombie goldfish wasn't much better than the non-minty kind.

"No offense, Frankie, I know you live in water and all, but you've got to shower more," I muttered.

Frankie actually gave me the fin-sign-language equivalent of "Talk to the fin, cos the face ain't listening."

Quickly I changed the subject. "Don't you think it's weird that Mark wanted to come on this camping weekend?" I said to Pradeep. "A few weeks ago he was calling it 'Moron Camp for Losers,' but now he wants to be here too."

"It's *very* weird," said Pradeep. "Do you think it could be part of some kind of evil plan?"

"I don't know," I replied, "but there's only one way to find out."

We pretended to be asleep when the leaders came around and checked the tents for lights out. Then we waited about another hour to make sure people would be snoozing before we headed out to see if Mark was up to anything evil.

We crawled on all fours between the tents. Pradeep had one of those cool head flashlights so he could crawl and see at the same time.

We'd put Frankie and some water in the clear plastic wallet that Pradeep's mom had put all his medical papers in. They're meant so that you can carry a map without it getting wet in

the rain, but it turns out that they're also perfect for carrying a zombie goldfish around your neck when you need your hands and feet to crawl.

When we got to Mark's tent, Pradeep turned off his head flashlight and we peered inside. The tent was empty! This was not a good sign.

We crawled in and Frankie's eyes started to glow bright green as we approached Mark's backpack, which was half spilt on the floor of the tent. His eyes lit up the stuff all over the floor. Most of it was typical camping stuff: T-shirts, socks and spare sneakers. But then the green glow lit up something white. I reached over and picked it up.

It was Mark's neatly folded Evil Scientist coat.

CHAPTER 6

A WHOLE TENT OF TROUBLE

"I knew it!" I whispered. "He's planning something."

Pradeep turned on his head flashlight again and found a copy of *Evil Scientist* magazine. He picked it up and thumbed through it. "Look, part of this page has been ripped out," he said.

I looked at the magazine. At the top of the ripped page was an ad:

CLASSIFIEDS   EVIL SCIENTIST

VACANCIES

EVIL SUMMER JOBS

Renowned Evil Scientist looking for Evil Assistant. Needs to show true Evil Attitude and Aptitude. No time-wasters.

Sinister castle for hire

BZZZ THING FOR SALE

"Do you think Mark's been job hunting in *Evil Scientist* magazine?" I asked.

"Maybe he's planning to do something this weekend to show his evil attitude and aptitude," Pradeep said. "Whatever he's plotting, it's not going to be good."

We heard a rustling outside. Pradeep switched off his head flashlight and I hid the plastic wallet inside my jacket to block the green light from Frankie's eyes. We dropped everything and crept away, just in case it was Mark coming back. I didn't feel like being pounded into the ground right now, and neither did Pradeep.

As soon as we were out of sight of Mark's tent I unzipped my jacket to let Frankie out. "Turn down the glow, Frankie," I whispered, as his eyes were still glowing brightly. "Someone might see you."

But if anything the glow got brighter. I didn't like it. Frankie's zombie sense was telling him something was wrong.

Then we saw the bushes just beyond our tent shake. Pradeep quickly pointed his head flashlight in that direction, expecting to catch Mark running away. But what we saw made us crawl faster than we had ever crawled in our lives. It was a pair of yellow eyes!

We scrambled into our tent and zipped up the flaps. By the light of Frankie's eyes and Pradeep's flashlight, we looked at the wreck that was our tent. The sleeping bags had been thrown around, the roll mats looked scratched, our clothes were all over the place and my secret stash of camping snacks was a pile of plastic bags and crumbs.

"Someone's been in here!" Pradeep said.

"Or some*thing*?" I added with a gulp.

Pradeep looked over at the wrappers and crumbs of Choco Crispy bars, chips and bread rolls. The only thing left was an unopened jar of peanut butter I had brought to make more sandwiches in case the campfire food was

yuck. "How much food did you have in here?" he asked.

"I don't know." I shrugged. "I get hungry. I was gonna share," I added.

"It's not that." Pradeep sighed, as if he was talking to his three-year-old sister, Sami. "You don't stash food in your tent, ever! It's rule number four of survival in the wild: 'In critters will creep, if you store food where you sleep.'"

I gave him a blank look. He continued, "If you keep food in your tent, animals will smell it and come looking for it."

"So you think that's what it was? An animal looking for food?" I said. "What if it was Mark looking for Frankie and he took the snacks as a kind of evil bonus?"

"He wasn't in his tent, true . . ." said Pradeep.

"But the eyes!" we both said at exactly the same time. We really need to stop doing that.

*

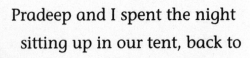

Pradeep and I spent the night sitting up in our tent, back to back, watching each set of tent flaps. Frankie acted as both nightlight and fishy bodyguard—ready to zombify anything that tried breaking in.

We didn't get much sleep.

When we heard the helicopter the next morning I think we both half dreamed that we were playing Army Chopper Air Race on the computer.

Frankie splashed me with a flick of his tail. "Huh? Wha . . . ?" I said, and scrambled out of the tent to see what was happening. Lots of people were up already and standing outside their tents. The chopper circled over the clearing. This was a different helicopter to yesterday though. It was bright yellow with black stripes and bold writing on the side that said: *Savage Safari.*

"Sam Savage!" I yelled at the same time as Pradeep crawled out of our tent. I zipped up my jacket again around the plastic wallet containing Frankie, suddenly realizing that my zombie goldfish necklace might not be great for anyone else to see.

The helicopter circled until most of the campers were out of their tents and looking up. As we were waiting for it to land I could hear lots of people talking about strange noises they had heard last night. Someone mentioned seeing animal tracks, and a couple of kids said they had heard movement outside their tents, as if something was crawling around the campsite.

Then a girl stood up and said that she saw some yellow eyes in the bushes outside her tent when she had looked out to see what the noise was.

Mark stepped forward. "I saw it too," he said, "whatever it was. I went outside my tent last night to—" he paused—"answer a call of nature . . ."

YOOOHOOO? IT'S NATURE CALLING!

Pradeep leaned toward me and whispered, "He means, 'Go for a pee.'"

Mark continued. "And there was definitely something in the bushes. When I went back inside my tent my stuff was all messed up. Something had been in there!"

Then we all heard a boy scream. He was standing right behind Pradeep and me, looking at the flaps to our tent. I hadn't noticed it last night, but there, right on the front, was what looked like a claw mark on the outer fabric of the flap. "It's the Beast of Burdock Woods!" he yelled. "It was here!"

CHAPTER 7

BREAKFAST AND THE BEAST

Grizzly came up and examined our tent flap.

"Don't worry, guppies!" he yelled over the noise of the chopper. "That doesn't mean there was a beast about! That could have caught on a branch blown in the wind. It was pretty gusty last night, and you've set up camp right next to some thorny bushes.

"Now let's give Sam Savage a Grizzly Woodland Camp welcome!" he said loudly to the whole camp as the helicopter finally landed. Soon the blades slowed to a standstill above the tiger-painted chopper.

Everyone clapped as Sam Savage stepped

out. He ducked below the blades and sauntered toward the crowd. He walked as if he could talk a tiger into lying down and being caught.

He looked exactly like he did on TV too. Safari hat, explorer clothes and his trademark monocle. There aren't many people who can rock a monocle. In fact, I think it's pretty much just him, but somehow, on Sam Savage, it works.

At first he just waved and smiled, but then his eyes caught a glimpse of something on the ground and he went into tracker mode, just like he does on TV when he gets a whiff of an animal's scent.

He walked over to a muddy patch on the ground and stared through his monocle at some animal tracks imprinted there.

"Interesting . . ." he said.

He followed the tracks while we all followed him around the camp. He picked up a tiny strand of black hair near another tent, bent down and sniffed the ground and then the air. The scent seemed to lead him to our tent. He looked at the scratch on the front flap.

"Good to see you, Sam," interrupted Grizzly, grabbing Sam's hand and pumping it up and down. "Listen, our campers are getting themselves all spooked about the so-called Beast of Burdock Woods," he went on. "You can tell them that it's all a bunch of hokum, right?"

"On the contrary," Sam Savage said, readjusting his monocle. "These signs lead me to believe that there is a 'beast,' or rather, a big cat, very near indeed." He looked at our shocked and scared faces.

Grizzly laughed and clapped Sam on the shoulder. "Good one, mate, you almost had me going there!" Then he turned to the assembled campers. "OK, mates, let's get some breakfast down before we start our 'Big Explore' with Sam Savage. Remember survival in the wild rule ninety-three: 'Morning food is your fuel *and* your survival tool.'"

Pradeep mouthed the words along with Grizzly.

"Head over to the chow line where the group leaders will serve you up some grub. And I promise there won't be any real grubs in it this time!" Grizzly got a laugh from the kids as they all started heading for the food tent.

But Pradeep, Frankie and I ducked down behind our tent so we could eavesdrop on Sam and Grizzly.

Grizzly turned to Sam. "Now, I know you want to put on a good show for the kids and all, Sam, but I think all that talk of a big cat is just gonna

spook 'em. Ease up on the melodrama a bit—this is meant to be fun for the guppies!"

Sam looked at Grizzly with serious eyes. Well, one serious eye and one serious monocle.

"I don't do melodrama." He leaned in to Grizzly. "By the end of today, I'm going to track and capture the so-called beast which is quite clearly loose in these woods—" he paused "—with or without your help. I suggest you keep the campers safe and out of my way."

Frankie thrashed hard in the bag that was still around my neck. I got the feeling he didn't like Sam Savage very much.

"You're going to be wasting your time tracking a fairy tale, mate." Grizzly shook his head and walked toward the food tent to join the rest of the campers. I thought about jumping up and telling Sam Savage what we had seen last night: the yellow eyes and the wrecked tent and how Pradeep and I both totally believed in the whole Beast of Burdock Woods thing, but then I saw

Mark walking over toward him.

Sam looked right at Mark as if he recognized him. "You've done well so far," he said.

"Cool," Mark replied.

Sam sniffed as if he'd smelled something bad and shook his head.

"I mean, um . . . I'm glad you're pleased, sir," Mark corrected himself.

"But you still have *much* more work to do if my contrivance is to reach fruition," Sam went on, rubbing his hands together in a totally evil way.

Mark gave him a blank stare.

"If the plan is going to work!" Sam snapped, cleaning his monocle with an embroidered silk hanky. "You're lucky the standard of applicants was so low, young man. Now get back to work!"

They shook hands and did a very quiet and formal "Mwhaa haaa haa haa" Evil Scientist laugh. Then Mark trudged off toward the food tent.

I shot Pradeep a look that said, "Sam Savage

is an Evil Scientist too? Whatever Mark and Sam are up to, we have to stop them!"

"Are you quite done with your eavesdropping?" a sharp voice said. We both raised our heads to see Sam Savage staring down at us through his monocle.

CHAPTER 8

SAVAGE BY NAME, SAVAGE BY NATURE

"Um, hello, Mr. Savage, sir," Pradeep said. He had turned on his best "talking to a teacher and showing lots of respect" voice. "I'm Pradeep and this is Tom," he added.

Sam Savage looked us up and down.

"Nice to meet you, but we should go and get in line for breakfast." I inched up the zipper on my jacket as I spoke so that he couldn't see any sign of Frankie underneath.

"And *why* were you both skulking behind this tent?" Sam said as he blocked our way.

"It's our tent," Pradeep chimed in right away. "We were just checking for any more claw marks."

"We think we saw the beast last night," I said. "Do you think it'll come back tonight?"

Sam Savage seemed to relax as soon as we mentioned the beast, as if he was back on camera again. "Tonight?" he said. "By tonight there won't be a beast to worry about." A little evil laugh escaped from his throat before he caught it and swallowed it down again. "Now, if you'll excuse me, I have to go and answer a call of nature."

I shot Pradeep a look that said, "That's exactly what Mark said earlier!"

"Um, nice meeting you, Mr. Savage," we both quickly mumbled, and hurried away.

"That was close," Pradeep said when we were a few feet away.

As we lined up for chow, I noticed that the guy serving up eggs had suddenly started staring at my fork and up my left nostril. Then he walked over to the bins and started picking out bits of moldy hot dog from the night before.

Frankie must have hypnotized him! I'd unzipped my jacket a bit when I came into the tent and Frankie must have wriggled the plastic wallet up just enough to peek out of the top.

"You just couldn't wait for me to ask, could you, Frankie?" I shook my head.

Frankie winked as the kitchen guy handed me a plate of moldy hot-dog bits and snapped out of his trance. He stared at his grubby hands.

"Um . . . line closed. I'll be back in a minute when I've washed up. Yuck!" he added.

"Great, so you get your breakfast but we have to wait," Pradeep whispered to Frankie.

"Lucky I still have some peanut butter left," I said, shoving Frankie back down into my jacket. "We can make sandwiches later." I grabbed some non-moldy toast from the bread baskets on the tables and we sat down.

But before we could swallow our first mouthful, we heard a scream outside.

Grizzly raced over, quickly followed by me

and Pradeep and loads of other campers.

I could see someone's hiking boots sticking out from the tall grass. Grizzly called for a first-aid kit and pushed the grass aside to reveal Mark lying on the ground. His shirt was torn with what looked like the same claw mark as on our tent flap. He looked as if he was just waking up.

"Mark?" I shouted.

He opened his eyes and glared at me for a second, then went back to looking hurt.

Grizzly helped him to sit up. "What happened, mate? Did you fall?"

"The beast. It attacked me," Mark whimpered.

Grizzly looked stunned. "Did any of you see anything?" he asked the other campers crowded around.

"No, we just heard a growl," a boy said.

"And then a scream. And then we came back and found him lying here," a girl added.

"Well, whatever happened, you seem to have come out of it without a scratch, it's just your shirt that's torn," Grizzly said to Mark. "We'd best get you checked out though, just in case."

Sam Savage walked over and stood at the center of the group of assembled kids. "You can't deny any longer that the so-called beast is out there," he called to Grizzly. "For the safety of the campers, we have to track and catch the beast!"

CHAPTER 9
THE EVIL CLAW

Grizzly looked down at Mark, then looked out at the rest of the campers. "OK guppies, back to the food tent for a regroup. The group leaders will teach you some indoor games and activities this morning." He looked over at Sam Savage. "Sam and I are going to track whatever did this."

I caught Mark shoot Sam Savage a look that said, "Was that good enough? Did it work?"

Mark's looks were so easy to read he might as well have been speaking out loud. In fact I think he actually mouthed the "Did it work?" bit.

Sam nodded.

While the rest of the campers were being

herded back to the food tent and Mark was being helped to the medical tent, Pradeep and I snuck off and headed for Mark's tent instead, to try to find out more about whatever Sam Savage and Mark were planning.

It was much easier to see everything in daylight. I picked up a metal-and-rubber shoe thing from the floor. "What's this?" I whispered to Pradeep.

"I'm not sure, but there's another one here," he said. Then he sat down on the floor and held it up to his foot. "It's made to fit over the top of a shoe." He turned it over and looked at the bottom. "Check this out." He held up the sole of the shoe, but instead of being like a normal trainer, the treads were in the shape of an animal footprint. They looked exactly like the tracks that Sam had been following around the camp earlier.

"So it was Mark who made the tracks last night?" I said.

I dug through Mark's backpack as I spoke and pulled out a really cool pair of night-vision goggles like they have in those nature shows on TV. I put them on.

"I guess this is how Mark could see last night when he was sneaking around pretending to be the beast. How do they look, Pradeep?"

Pradeep turned around and gasped. "The yellow eyes!" he said. "The goggles have got yellow eyes painted on them!"

I slipped them off to see for myself. So now we knew that Mark was tricking everyone into believing that there was a Beast of Burdock Woods. And that Sam Savage was probably in on it too. But was Mark really just doing all this just to get a summer job as an Evil Assistant?

As I put the goggles back where I found them, I noticed a torn page of a magazine had fallen out of the backpack.

I read it aloud: "Take your first steps toward world domination. Earn enough money in one summer to get the Evil Scientist lair you've always dreamed of. With Evil Scientist Assistant and Apprentice schemes you can do it! Do you have what it takes? Call Sam Savage to apply . . ."

"That must be the missing page from *Evil Scientist* magazine," Pradeep said.

"So Mark's working for Sam Savage to earn enough money to build an evil lair!" I replied. "But that still doesn't explain why Sam is out there right now, tracking a fake Beast of Burdock Woods."

"Maybe Mark will spill the beans if

we confront him," Pradeep suggested. "I mean, maybe he will just tell us, if we ask him," he explained.

"We can't take Frankie near Mark," I said. "He'll just zombie-fish-attack him in front of everyone."

"OK," said Pradeep. "I have a plan. I'll take Frankie back to our tent and put him in one of the water containers or something so he's safe. You go and find Mark. Take this as evidence," he added, putting one of the animal-print shoes in my backpack.

I lifted the plastic wallet over my head, but as I did Frankie jumped out, bit the sleeve of my jacket and wouldn't let go.

"I know you want to come and help, Frankie, but we can't risk it," I said to him. He shook his head and held on tight.

Pradeep took a clear plastic bag out of a mini Evil Scientist chemistry set we found in Mark's backpack and filled it with water from his canteen.

"Frankie, if we get the information out of Mark, then we can stop Sam Savage doing whatever evil plan he's planning on doing!" I said.

Pradeep held out the bag for Frankie to jump into and Frankie looked up at me. "I promise you can come with us when we go looking for Sam later," I said. "Deal?"

Frankie held out a fin for a fin-slap high five, then somersaulted into the plastic bag of water.

Pradeep and Frankie headed off while I ran to the medical tent, but when I got there Mark was gone.

One of the group leaders was tidying up some bandages. "Mark? The kid who had the 'claw mark' on him?" he asked. "He was sent back to his tent. Why?"

"Um, just checking he's OK," I said.

"He's fine," he answered. "In fact, when we checked his bag we found a garden tool that he had clearly used to make the scratch on his shirt

look like an animal attack. Now Sam Savage and Grizzly Cook are out there wasting a whole morning tracking something that this kid made up. I'm sure they'll call his parents when they get back."

"OK, well, thanks," I said. "I'll just get back to the food tent then," I lied, crossing my fingers behind my back.

I need to tell Pradeep, I thought as I raced back to our tent.

But when I opened the zipper, the first thing I spotted was Pradeep stuffed into a sleeping bag with only his head sticking out and a rope tied around the outside of the bag! His mouth was taped up with Band-Aids that Mark must have taken from the medical tent.

The second thing I spotted was that the plastic bag with Frankie in it was gone!

CHAPTER 10
TO TRACK THE TRACKER

"Marmks moot . . . Ouch! . . . Frankie!" Pradeep said as I unstuck the Band-Aids over his mouth. "He headed off into the woods after Sam Savage and Grizzly Cook!"

I untied the rope and Pradeep wriggled free from his sleeping bag. "We have to go after them!" I said.

We both reckoned that Mark would be way easier to track than Grizzly Cook or Sam Savage. They would both move stealthily through the woods. Mark would blunder along, stomping on plants and breaking twigs with every step.

Pradeep grabbed his backpack and I threw my jacket, flashlight and the remaining jar of peanut butter into mine. You never knew when you'd need some peanut-butter energy!

We had to use all our patented Secret Stealth Escape Strategies to get out of the camp without being seen:

1. Blending into the surroundings . . .

2. Diversion tactics . . .

3. Aerial acrobatics (because people never look up).

When we finally made it to the edge of camp, Pradeep led the way into the woods. We were probably walking for at least half an hour before I got out the peanut butter and had a fingerful of "fuel," as Grizzly would say. Pradeep was up ahead, working out which route to take.

That's when I heard a very strange sound. It was a low rumbling, like the sound my belly makes before lunch, but as if someone had a microphone up to my belly at the time. I know what that sounds like because I did that once in the music room at school to see what amplified belly rumbling was like. And it was exactly like the sound I heard then.

"Pradeep," I whispered. "Listen."

He stopped and turned around. Then I heard a twig snap and rustling in the bushes behind me. I ran over to where Pradeep was standing. "There's something hiding in the bushes!" I hissed.

"It must be Mark," Pradeep whispered. "He

probably heard us and decided to hide until we went past and then scare us." Pradeep raised his voice to a shout. "But we aren't scared of a little rustling in the bushes, are we?"

That's when I saw a pair of yellow eyes peering out from under the thick bushes.

"Look, Pradeep, it's the night-vision goggles," I whispered. "We're on to you, Mark," I yelled, raising my voice. "We know that you faked the whole Beast of Burdock Woods thing, so just give up and come out now!"

We heard another growl. "Yeah, great sound effects, Mark," I went on. "You sound more like Mrs. Roger's old tabby than a big cat." I smiled proudly at my awesome insult. "Now cut it out and give us back Frankie before you get into any more trouble."

I walked back toward the bushes and the growl got louder.

Suddenly Pradeep grabbed my shoulder. "Don't go any closer."

"Why? We've got him!" I whispered back. "Plus, I'm really liking having one up on Mark for a change."

Pradeep pointed to the paw-prints on the ground. They were fresh and led over to the bush where the growls had come from. "So, Mark must have used his shoe things again to make the tracks. *And?*" I said.

Pradeep pulled one of the shoe things out of his backpack at the same time as I remembered that the other was in mine.

"Maybe he has a spare pair," I said hopefully, just before we shot each other a look that said, "GULP!"

CHAPTER 11

WILL THE REAL BEAST PLEASE STAND UP?

Every cell in my body wanted to run, but Pradeep pointed to the tree just next to us. It had low branches we could reach, and we were both expert tree climbers.

Pradeep counted silently on his fingers: one, two . . . On "three" we both jumped for the tree.

When we were about three or four branches up we looked down and couldn't believe our eyes.

Emerging from the undergrowth was a sleek black cat. It looked about the size of a Labrador dog, but definitely didn't have that "Here, boy, go fetch" look about it. It stared right at us with its yellow eyes and it licked its lips.

"It's a panther, I think," Pradeep said.

"Oh, good.
I'm glad I'll
at least
know
what's
eating
me,"
I said.
"What are we
going to do?"

The panther sniffed the air and then prowled toward our tree.

"I think it smells something," Pradeep whispered. "Did you bring any food with you?"

"Just the peanut butter," I said. Then I remembered something. "Yesterday evening, when we were walking to the campsite, I had peanut-butter sandwiches on me," I said.

"And you also had one when we were by the stream with Frankie and we saw the yellow eyes," Pradeep replied.

"But wouldn't a panther rather eat some child-sized red meat than a sandwich?" I asked.

"My gran's cat loves peanut butter," Pradeep said. "She'll do anything for it. I wonder if this big cat likes it too. Maybe that's why she's following us." He pulled a pinecone off the tree we were in and motioned for me to pass him the peanut butter. Then he dunked the pine-cone into the jar, covering it with delicious peanut goo.

The panther put her paws up on the tree and stretched up to catch the smell.

"Um, Pradeep, hate to worry you, but I'm pretty sure that panthers can climb trees," I squeaked.

Pradeep tossed the peanut-butter-coated pinecone a little way away and the panther ran over to it and immediately started licking it

and batting it around with her paws.

"She looks young to me . . ." said Pradeep thoughtfully. "Not that I'm an expert on panther age or anything. I guess she's more like a panther kitten really."

"Well, that panther kitten could still have us as a main course after her peanut-butter starter!" I said. "We've got to get out of here, find Mark, save Frankie and warn Grizzly about the panther!"

Pradeep collected more pinecones and spread them with peanut butter too.

"What are you doing?" I asked.

"Look." Pradeep got the cat's attention by dangling a peanut-butter-flavored pinecone near her so she could smell it. Then he chucked it over into the bushes where she had been hiding before. She raced after it right away.

"Now!" Pradeep whispered, and we quietly climbed down the tree and ran in the opposite direction, following what must have been

Mark's trail into the woods.

Every so often Pradeep would throw one of the peanut-butter-coated pinecones as far back as he could along the trail, so that the panther would stop to lick the peanut butter instead of trying to eat us!

Soon we reached a large clearing and spotted the tiger-painted *Savage Safari* helicopter camouflaged by branches and leaves. "I guess Sam Savage wants to be able to make a quick getaway," Pradeep said.

On the other side of the clearing from where we stood was a small canvas tent. As we approached I could hear the distinctive "Mwhaa haaa haa haa" of two Evil Scientists coming from inside.

"Hey, Pradeep, why do you think there's a rope circle around this unexpectedly large pile of leaves we're standing in?" I started to say. What actually came out was, "Hey, Pradeep, why do you think . . . Arrrrrgggggghhhh!" as we suddenly

both found ourselves swinging by our ankles
high above the ground.

CHAPTER 12

THE OLD ROPE-BOOBY-TRAP-IN-A-PILE-OF-LEAVES TRICK

The sound of our "Arrrrrggggghhhh!" and the whoosh of ropes must have grabbed the attention of Sam Savage and Mark pretty quickly.

Sam appeared first, dragging Grizzly Cook with him. Grizzly's arms were tied to his sides and there was a rope around his wrists too.

"I told you they would show up eventually," sneered Sam to Grizzly. Then to us he said, "So nice of you to swing by!" He wheezed out another evil laugh as we swung upside down, staring at them. Then he pushed Grizzly roughly to the ground.

"I should never have trusted you, Sam." Grizzly

shook his head. "You must have been faking your TV show for years. You couldn't track a lion in your living room!" Looking up at our upside-down faces he whispered, "I'm sorry you got dragged into this, guppies." Then he pulled on the ropes around his hands and gave us a knowing wink and a nod. From above I could see that he had picked up a piece of flint from the ground where Sam had thrown him, and had started to saw away at his rope ties.

"I don't need to track animals anymore," spat Sam Savage. "The challenge has gone out of it. I've caught and stuffed pretty much every dangerous animal on the planet, or at least my staff has! But to capture this particular rare creature, I needed some kind of fake dangerous animal as a distraction, and the so-called Beast of Burdock Woods was the perfect ruse!" He smirked.

Then Mark came out of the tent carrying a jar with Frankie in it. Frankie was green-eyed with

rage. He thrashed against the sides and pushed at the lid on the jar. "Hey, morons, nice of you to swing by!" Mark guffawed at his own joke.

"We've already done that joke!" snapped Sam.

"But at least you have been useful for one thing. You have brought me my prize catch. In all my years of tracking deadly animals, I've never caught and stuffed a zombie goldfish. As soon as you told me of its existence in your Evil Assistant application letter, I knew I had to have it." He pulled a folded piece of paper out of his white coat pocket and held it up. It was a drawing of Frankie with zombie eyes.

Pradeep and I struggled to free our feet from the ropes. "You can't keep Frankie!" Pradeep shouted.

"And you can't stuff him either," I yelled. "We won't let you!"

Mark and Sam both laughed again.

"And how, exactly, are you going to stop us?" asked Sam with a raised eyebrow.

"Frankie, zombify him now!" I shouted. "Before it's too late!"

"You foolish children," said Sam, adjusting his monocle. "My Evil Assistant warned me of the fish's power, so I brought a hypno-proof jar to hold him in. I am the great Sam Savage, after all. I didn't get this far by not being prepared."

"You're gonna be prepared . . . as a panther snack," I yelled, still struggling to free my foot.

"Good insult," said Pradeep, then turned to Sam. "Look, you've got to let us down. The Beast of Burdock Woods isn't a fake, it's real. And it's following us. It could be here at any second!"

"And I *really* don't want to be hanging around on a rope like a giant cat toy when it does turn up," I added.

"Nice try, moron. Like we're gonna fall for that." Mark laughed. "I was the Beast of Burdock Woods. And I totally rocked at it too."

"Now you get to see your precious zombie goldfish get stuffed," Sam Savage snarled. "Evil Assistant, get the video camera. I want this moment recorded."

Mark handed the jar with Frankie in it to Sam and went back into the tent for the camera.

Grizzly took the opportunity to pounce.

In less than a second he had kicked Sam's legs out from under him, sending both Sam and the hypno-proof jar to the ground. The jar shattered and Frankie leaped onto Sam's face and tail-slapped him, while Grizzly ran over to the booby trap and got me and Pradeep down. We landed with a thud in the pile of dried leaves below.

As Grizzly helped us to our feet he said, "Good distraction technique, talking about the Beast of Burdock Woods. That gave me the

time I needed to cut through my ropes."

"We weren't joking about the beast," I said to Grizzly.

At that moment we heard a loud growl behind us.

CHAPTER 13

THE RETURN OF THE BEAST

The Beast of Burdock Woods appeared from the trees with a pinecone in her mouth. She padded toward Frankie and Sam, dropping the pinecone as she slunk through the grass, ready to pounce. She had a new scent in her nostrils. Fish!

Frankie leaped off Sam's face and jumped into a nearby puddle. His zombie senses must have alerted him to the danger. Sam sat up and found himself face-to-face with the big cat in full hunting mode!

"Jitterbugging jackrabbits!" Grizzly cried. "It *is* real!" He rubbed his eyes. "OK, boys, stay still. Don't do anything that might spook her."

Just then Mark came out of the tent. As soon as he saw the big cat though, he dropped the camera and ran.

"Arghhhhhhhhhh!" he cried as he disappeared into the trees.

"No! Don't run!" Grizzly shouted, but it was too late. The cat gave chase and soon she was right on Mark's heels.

"We've got to save him!" I shouted, scooping Frankie up from the puddle. Pradeep and I ran after Mark, and Grizzly ran after us, leaving Sam sitting alone in the mud.

We caught up with Mark and the panther a few minutes later. Mark was up a tree that leaned out at an angle over a stream, and the panther was pawing at him.

"Argggghhhh! Get it away! Get it away!" Mark was shouting.

"We've got to find a way to catch the cat," Grizzly whispered to Pradeep, looking around for anything he could use to make a trap.

I looked down at Frankie. He was gasping for breath and needed water. Gently I slipped him into the burbling water upstream of the tree where the big cat was stalking Mark.

"Frankie," I whispered, "I know you don't exactly like Mark . . ." Frankie spat a glob of water in Mark's direction. "OK, I know you *really* don't like Mark, but he's my brother and I don't really want him to be eaten by a panther. Can you help?"

Frankie rolled his eyes, shook his head and folded his fins stubbornly.

"Please," I begged.

Frankie's eyes glowed green, then he flipped backward and in a flash of orange scales sped away toward the overhanging tree.

Grizzly and Pradeep were hard at work. Grizzly had been impressed to find Pradeep had twelve pairs of socks in his backpack. They were tying some together and stretching them over a large Y-shaped branch to make a slingshot.

The panther was now actually climbing the tree. It was out over the water and creeping closer and closer to Mark. Just then, Frankie jumped up out of the water and splashed the panther with his tail.

"*Rawwwwwallll!*" the panther growled as Frankie dropped back into the water.

He had got her attention! The big cat leaned over the tree trunk and swiped at Frankie as he leaped out of the water again. She clawed at him as water splashed her face. Frankie was in full zombie fish mode now. His eyes glowed

green as he leaped up for his third splash at the big cat. That's when she caught him off guard.

Her left claw caught his tail fin. She had hooked her fish and was lifting him up to her mouth!

We only had seconds. I grabbed a pinecone from the ground and put it in the slingshot Pradeep and Grizzly had made. Pradeep and I pulled back together and sent it flying at the panther.

It hit her right on the nose before she could take a nibble of zombie fish. She growled at us but didn't let her catch go. She lifted her paw a second time to drop Frankie into her mouth, but as she did so, for a split second she looked Frankie in the eye. That was all it took.

When she turned back to face Mark again, she was looking at the tree trunk with one eye and up Mark's left nostril with the other. Frankie was sitting on the panther's nose staring back at her.

"In all my years in the wild, I've never seen a fish take on a panther before. Let alone win!" Grizzly scratched his head.

"Whoaaaa, dude! The cat has the zombie stare. How did he do that?" said Mark. Then he got that evil glint back in his eyes. "Cool. Now the beast is busted I can take the fish back to Sam and ace my evil job. I'll have the money to build an evil lair in no time!"

In one move Mark grabbed Frankie, covering

his eyes, and jumped into the stream. He floated on the current as it raced back toward the clearing and Sam Savage.

"Frankie!" I yelled.

"Mwah ha ha ha glug, ughhh!" drifted back to us over the sound of the rushing water.

"I know the route of this stream," Grizzly said. "It snakes around a bit, so if we go direct we might get to the clearing before he does."

The panther was still in the tree, only now it was looking down at my backpack and up Grizzly's left nostril.

"But what do we do with the Beast of Burdock Woods?" Pradeep asked.

CHAPTER 14

ZOMBIE BEAST ON THE PROWL

"We can't leave her here," Grizzly said. He spoke softly as he went up to the panther and gently picked her up and put her around his shoulders. Then the three of us ran through the woods to the clearing.

"Hopefully we've got here before Mark," said Grizzly as we reached the edge of the stream near the clearing. "Quick, hide in those bushes."

Pradeep and I dived into the bushes on our left. Grizzly laid the panther down on the ground in front of the bushes we were hiding behind. He positioned her so that her face was looking away from the water.

The panther's eyes gazed both at the bush and up my left nostril.

"How are you boys at growls?" Grizzly said.

Pradeep and I both shot him a look that said, "We have a wide range of animal growls. What sort would you prefer?"

Grizzly smiled. "I'll leave it up to you," he said, and jumped behind a bush on the opposite side of the track.

A few seconds later we heard Mark splashing about in the rushing water. "Get back here you slippery little . . . guurrrrrggggh!" he gurgled.

I peered out. Mark was trying to keep hold of a very slippery Frankie as he kept slurping out of Mark's clutch, only to be caught again. Eventually Mark floundered onto the bank of the stream and stood up with Frankie trapped in his cupped hands.

Now was our chance.

Pradeep let off his most terrifying imitation-panther growl from behind the bush.

Mark looked over and saw the big cat sitting there. Right on cue he screamed and threw his hands in the air, sending Frankie flying backward. We could see flashes of orange and heard little fishy "umph" noises as Frankie ricocheted off a couple of branches, bounced off Grizzly's face and then somersaulted neatly into one of Pradeep's water-filled sick bags that I was holding at the ready.

Grizzly jumped out with a rope he had made out of Pradeep's socks and looped it around Mark. "Gotcha!" he cried as he pinned Mark's arms to his sides.

"Sam!" yelled Mark, but before he could get out another word Pradeep shoved a balled-up sock in his open mouth. "Put a sock in it, Mark!" he said triumphantly. Then he added, "It is clean. Just so you know."

At that moment we heard the helicopter engine start up.

"Sam Savage is making a getaway!" Pradeep

shouted over the roar of the helicopter blades.

While Grizzly finished tying up Mark, Pradeep and I ran for the chopper. It was hovering a little way above the ground when we got there.

"It's too late, he's getting away," Pradeep said.

Then I spotted the sock-and-stick slingshot sticking out of Pradeep's backpack.

I shot Pradeep a look that explained my plan. The upside was that Sam's chopper had open sides so we had a good chance if we were brave enough to take it. The downside was that if we missed, Frankie might end up in the chopper blades as zombie sushi.

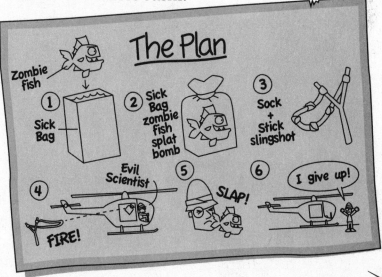

"It's too risky for Frankie," Pradeep said.

"You're right." I sighed. Sam Savage was going to get away after all.

Frankie splashed me and I looked down at him in his sick bag. His eyes were a wild bright green. He turned toward the helicopter and nodded.

"Are you sure?" I asked him.

Frankie winked, and waved a fin as if to say, "Let's go!"

I scrunched down the top of the bag to make a zombie fish splat bomb and Pradeep readied the slingshot.

As we pulled back the socks and aimed at Sam's monocle, we counted, "One, two, three . . . bombs away!"

CHAPTER 15

SPLAT-BOMB SAVAGE

The splat bomb sailed through the air toward
the chopper as if in slow motion. I shut my eyes
as the sick bag flew toward its spinning blades.

SPLAT! The bomb had hit its mark, knocking
Sam's monocle clean off, splattering him with
water, and delivering a very angry zombie
goldfish to do some serious kung fu fish-slapping.

In a flash Grizzly raced past us, pulled himself
up using the helicopter skids, and climbed into
the copilot seat. He expertly landed the chopper,
turned off the engine, and the blades finally
started to slow.

Sam fell out of the other side of the helicopter,

still fighting with Frankie. "You ridiculous green-eyed goldfish!" he shouted between fishy slaps. "Don't you know who I am?"

As they rolled on the ground near the edge of the stream, the panther approached. She still had the zombie stare so Frankie must have been controlling her as she stalked toward Sam with an intimidating "Grrrrrr!"

Sam sat up and backed away toward the water. He'd managed to wrestle Frankie off his face now and had trapped him in his hands.

"You would have looked lovely stuffed and mounted on my wall, fish, but if I can't have you, no one will!" he screamed. And with that he hurled Frankie into the stream.

Pradeep and I ran to the edge of the water. But there was no sign of Frankie's green eyes or orange scales.

I reached in and dug around with my hands, hoping to grab hold of him. But Grizzly pulled me back. "Not so fast, mate. Around that next bend the current really picks up. There's a weir and then the stream goes underground for miles and miles. You don't want to end up in there."

I looked over at Pradeep and Grizzly. I didn't know what a weir was, but it didn't sound good.

Pradeep caught my look. "It's like a waterfall," he explained. "Frankie will probably be OK if he goes over. But if he gets sucked into the underground stream, we might never see him again!"

"We've got to save him," I cried.

Grizzly kept hold of my shoulder and wouldn't let go. "Ya can't go in after him," he said firmly. "I'm sorry."

Then the panther started moving slowly toward the water. It dabbed its paw into the stream, then shook it out. Then it ran back and jumped in.

"I didn't know panthers could swim," Pradeep said.

"There are lots of big cats that love the water," said Grizzly, "but I've never heard of one diving in to save a fish before!"

Pradeep and I ran along the bank of the stream while Grizzly tied up Sam with even more of Pradeep's spare socks. We could see the panther up ahead. She was doggy-paddling (which in future I'm going to call "panther-paddling") through the churning water. The top of the weir was just yards away!

Then we saw a flash of green and the flick of an orange fin right in the middle of the stream by some rocks.

"He's over there," I shouted.

Frankie looked tired. He kept flinging himself up out of the water, but the current always pushed him back. Grizzly had caught up with us and looked on.

The panther swam over and clung to the

rocks with her front paws as the crashing white water drummed against her. She couldn't let go of the rock to swipe Frankie up though, or they might both end up over the weir and be sucked underground.

With one last effort, Frankie leaped up out of the water and toward the panther's open mouth.

CHAPTER 16

FRANKIE SNACK

The panther caught Frankie in her mouth in one scoop.

"She ate Frankie!" Pradeep cried.

"I think she's just holding him in her mouth, like mother crocodiles do with their young," said Grizzly.

The panther pushed herself up and out of the foaming water so she was standing on the rocks. Then she leaped across from stone to stone, heading upstream. When she reached calmer waters she swam to the shore.

We were there to meet her when she climbed out of the water.

Grizzly got out his canteen and held it to the panther's mouth. Frankie slid down her tongue and plopped into the water.

"Wow, that goldfish is one serious survivor," Grizzly exclaimed, wiping his brow.

"We'd better get back to check on Mark and Sam Savage," I said.

"Did you use a triple hornbench smuggler's knot on them both?" Pradeep asked Grizzly.

Grizzly smiled. "The old knots are the best."

When we got back to the clearing, Mark started shouting "Met mit maway mom meee!" at the panther through his sock gag.

Sam was muttering to himself too. "A fish? I was defeated by a couple of kids and a fish!" He got more and more worked up until he was shouting, "I'll ruin you, Grizzly! If you report this and turn me in, then no one will ever come on one of your survival camps ever again!"

Suddenly Frankie leaped out of the canteen and onto Sam's face. He stared into his one

eye and one monocle. In a second Sam was mumbling "Swishy little fishy," and staring up my left nostril and at the side of the helicopter. Frankie jumped back into the canteen.

"What did the fish do to him?" Grizzly asked, pulling the sock out of Mark's mouth.

"Man, he zombified my boss," Mark grumbled.

"Is that what he did to the panther too?" Grizzly turned to Pradeep and me.

We nodded.

"Wow," said Grizzly, looking impressed.

"It's kinda natural behavior for a zombie goldfish," Pradeep added. "Well, at least for Frankie anyway. It's not like we know any other zombie fish."

We all looked over at the panther. "What's going to happen to her?" I asked.

"We can't leave her out here, that's for sure," Grizzly replied.

"I've got an idea. Maybe Sam can do something for her after all." I looked at Pradeep.

"Yeah." He nodded. "With Frankie's help."

I whispered our plan to Frankie and in a minute he was back balancing on Sam's nose, looking into his eyes again.

Then Sam started talking in regular words that didn't include "swishy fish" but also didn't involve anything evil. Quickly Pradeep and I untied his sock ropes.

"Oh, what a lovely big cat!" Sam said, stroking the panther. "I feel an overwhelming urge to

start an animal sanctuary with all my money, and retire from television."

"Man, I totally just lost my summer job," Mark whined.

"Right, everyone in the helicopter now. We're heading back to camp in style," Grizzly said.

Sam and Mark sat in the back with the panther lying between them.

Sam was now muttering, "Pretty little kitty," over and over, and scratching the panther behind the ears. Mark was looking like . . . well, like he was trapped in the back of a helicopter with a zombified panther, really. It's a pretty specific look.

"And you two can sit up front and see what it's like to fly one of these," Grizzly added.

Frankie peered up out of the canteen.

"Oh yes, I haven't forgotten about you." Grizzly pulled out a clear plastic bottle and poured the canteen water and Frankie into it.

Then he wedged it between the windshield of the helicopter and the dashboard controls. "There you go. Best bird's-eye view that a fish has ever had, I bet."

CHAPTER 17

THE FLYING ZOMBIE

Frankie loved flying. Pradeep and I loved it too, even though Pradeep was glad he'd brought his sick bags. But the best bit was watching the whole camp gather to see Grizzly land the chopper and then watch us get out with the panther on a lead made from a rope of Pradeep's socks.

Grizzly put the panther in a pen and Frankie unzombified her. She stayed really calm though. And we gave her a couple of peanut-butter pinecones to lick on. Later that afternoon some people from Sam Savage's new wildlife sanctuary came to pick up Sam and the panther.

There was a lady with a clipboard with them.

She held out a picture of a panther cub as she spoke to Grizzly. "There was an old, rich recluse who lived on the other side of these woods. He used to collect all kinds of exotic animals, including this little panther cub. Unfortunately the man died last year. She must have escaped and been roaming wild in the woods ever since."

Grizzly smiled. "She sure looked like a survivor to me."

"It's good that you were able to trap her. It's not a very safe place for a young panther," she replied.

"Well, I didn't really do the tracking on this one. And neither did Sam Savage. It was all down to these two young fellows here, Tom and Pradeep," Grizzly said.

Pradeep and I stood a whole head taller when he said that. The other campers looked impressed as Grizzly continued: "They sure have a knack for wilderness survival and for looking after animals. Not to mention saving our skins as well while you were at it," he added with a wink.

The lady took a couple of pictures of Pradeep and me with Grizzly.

After Grizzly made Mark apologize to the other campers and leaders, he handed him a letter. The front read: "Summer Apprenticeship with Sam Savage."

"Can't cut out on a job half done, can ya, mate?" Grizzly said to Mark. "That wouldn't be the Grizzly Woodland Explorer way." Pradeep and I peeked around Mark's shoulder to read it. The letter was from Sam's new wildlife sanctuary, thanking Mark for volunteering to clean out the big-cat enclosures every weekend over the summer.

"The best way to learn the difference between being a fake wild animal and

respecting a real one is cleaning up after them."
Grizzly grinned. "You won't make that mistake
again."

"Man, this is like the worst failed evil plan
ever!" Mark moaned.

That evening was epic! We sat around the
campfire and Grizzly, Pradeep and I told the
other campers about how we tracked the panther
and saved Mark and Sam Savage. The lady with
the clipboard took notes about our adventure
and the photographer took some more pictures
around the fire.

The campers "Ooohed" and "Ahhhed" as
we held up the slingshot made out of Pradeep's
socks. We left out the bits about Frankie being a
zombie goldfish and Sam and Mark being Evil
Scientists and stuff. Now that Sam was going to
help the panther and other animals, there didn't
seem much point blowing his cover.

"So what would you say was your secret to

tracking the big cat?" the lady with the clipboard said, writing everything down. "This could be good press for the sanctuary."

"Ummm, peanut butter," Pradeep replied. "Oh yeah, and clean socks. You can never have too many pairs of clean socks."

She looked at us both with a slightly strange expression, but kept writing.

"Oh, and a fish!" I added. The plastic water bottle that Frankie was in sloshed from side

to side and Frankie peeked his head out the top. "We couldn't have done it without one very brave fish."

REVENGE OF THE PARANORMAL PETS

CHAPTER 1

THE MISSING-PETS MYSTERY

Frankie, my pet zombie goldfish, jumped out of the jar of green watercolor paint and flopped onto the paper that Sami, Pradeep's little sister, was holding. He made a slimy green semicircle and then leaped back into the pot.

Sami wiped her hands on her sparkly mermaid outfit that was already coated in green paint. "Yaaay! Fishy do shell!" She clapped. "Now fishy do feet?"

Frankie peered out of the top of the paint pot and looked at me.

"We did say we'd help Sami make the missing-tortoise posters," I said to him.

Frankie sighed and shrugged his shoulders. Actually I'm pretty sure goldfish don't have shoulders, but there was a definite shrugging of something. He flung himself out of the pot again and splashed the paper with his tail four times underneath the semicircle he had already made. I had to admit, for a goldfish he had pretty good artistic flair.

Frankie turned into a zombie goldfish when Pradeep and I shocked him back to life with a battery after my Evil Scientist big brother, Mark, tried to murder him with toxic gunk. Ever since then, Frankie has mostly been into trying to get

Mark back by kung fu fish-slapping and hypnotizing people. I didn't get to see his artistic side much. It made a nice change.

Pradeep sat typing away on his laptop at our kitchen table. He looked down at the wet poster on our kitchen floor. "Wow, that really does look like Toby, our cousin's tortoise. Good job, Frankie!"

Frankie waved his fin in thanks and then jumped into the water bucket to swish all the paint off his scales.

Sami held up one of the posters.

"Tom, you write one more word?" Sami asked.

"Sure," I said, picking up the marker pen again, "if it helps find Toby."

MISSING

Toby the tortoise
Last seen Saturday

"Toby telepopping tortoise!" she said in her "I'm being serious even though I know this sounds very cute" voice.

I shot Pradeep a look to see if he could translate.

"She means 'teleporting tortoise.'" He smiled. "Our cousin Joe always said that Toby must be able to teleport because he can be right behind you one second and the next he's clear across the garden, heading for the fence."

"Has Toby run away before?" I asked.

"Yeah," Pradeep said, "but not since they fixed the fence." He clicked on the keyboard of the laptop again. "I just hope we find him before Joe gets back from holiday tomorrow. All we had to do was watch him for the weekend and feed him a bit of lettuce now and then." Pradeep sighed. "I shouldn't have let Sami take him out in the garden."

"Toby telepopped bye-bye," Sami said, and kissed the little green painted tortoise on the poster. Which of course made her lips green. At least they matched the rest of her.

"Any luck on that lost-pets website?" I asked

as I squeezed the word 'teleporting' on to the posters.

"I've been searching on Pet Find, Where's My Pet.com and something called Paranormal Pet Link, but nothing has come up," Pradeep said, closing the laptop. "There seem to be lots of other local pets missing too. Some of them for a few days or more. Cats, hamsters, rabbits, snakes . . . even some rare birds." Then he looked at Sami. "But I'm sure Toby will turn up soon. Let's get the posters up around the neighborhood and maybe someone will spot him."

"Frankie, do you want to come and put up posters?" I said, lifting up the bucket that was now filled with greenish water. An orange face peered up at me. Frankie shook his head, splashing me, and dived back under the green liquid, blowing bubbles across the surface.

"I think he just likes swimming around in that green water and doesn't want to get back in his bowl," Pradeep said.

"OK," I said to Frankie. "I'll put some bath toys in the bucket with you and you can pretend you're stalking the rubber ducky again if you want."

"Mark's out and we'll only be gone a few minutes anyway," Pradeep said. "Frankie'll be fine."

We headed out of the kitchen door with a roll of tape and the posters, ready to hit the trees and lampposts along our street. But what we saw made us stop in our tracks.

CHAPTER 2

AN AWFULLY "NICE" EVIL PLOT

Pradeep and I looked at each other. I had never seen so many missing-pet posters in all my life. Every lamppost and tree was already covered in pictures of missing kittens, rabbits, birds, snakes, gerbils, lizards, stick insects and guinea pigs.

Then one poster caught my eye.

I pulled the magic marker I had used on our posters out of my pocket and wrote the number on my arm.

MISSING!
LEVITATING BUDGIE

Possible victim of
Evil Kidnap Plot!
Any info call 632 096 0361

Then I shot Pradeep a look that said, "If there's an evil kidnap plot, then you know who has to be behind it!"

"This has Mark written all over it," Pradeep's look answered.

Mark's Evil Scientist track record is pretty much one hundred percent for being behind all the evil plots we've ever uncovered—from toxic-gunking Frankie and trying to flush him to taking over the school or faking wild-animal attacks and hypnotizing TV stars. When you think about it, he's had a pretty busy evil year so far.

We grabbed Sami and raced back home. As we neared the kitchen door I screeched to a halt and whispered to Pradeep, "What if Mark is in there now? What if he's after Frankie? Maybe he's been waiting all day for us to go out so he can sneak in and grab him? We have to use the element of surprise!"

Pradeep and Sami nodded.

Pradeep counted down silently using his fingers. Then on zero or "fist with no fingers up," we stormed through the kitchen door and Sami shouted, "Surprise!"

"Um . . . that's not quite what we meant, Sami," Pradeep started to whisper, before realizing that Mark *was* in the kitchen after all.

"What's with all the missing pets?" I yelled. "We know you have something to do with it, so you'd better confess now!"

At the same time as I yelled this I noticed something was definitely wrong. Mark was wearing his white Evil Scientist coat, but instead of threatening to pummel us into the ground, like he usually did, he was sitting at the kitchen table quietly drinking a cup of tea!

He set his teacup down gently on its saucer.

"Good morning, Tom," he said with a smile. "Good morning, Pradeep." Then he turned and grinned down at Sami, who stared at him as if he had just landed from Planet Zog. "And how are you today, you little cutie-wootie?"

Sami squeaked and hid behind Pradeep's leg.

I immediately checked the bucket to see if Frankie was OK. He was thrashing around in the green water as if he was upset, but he wasn't jumping out and trying to zombie thrash Mark like he normally did. Something was *really* wrong here. It was as if we'd walked into a parallel dimension where Mark and Frankie didn't hate each other. Urggghh!

"I don't know what you're up to, Mark," said Pradeep suspiciously, "but where are the pets?"

"I'm very sorry, but I don't know what you mean," Mark said. "But you all look very upset. Shall I make you a soothing cup of tea?"

Pradeep and I shot each other a look that said, "If he's bluffing, then he's a lot better at it than he used to be!"

"Mark, it's no use trying to fool us. We know what you're up to," I said.

"Yeah, I mean you even have on your Evil

Scientist coat!" Pradeep added. "Your outfit gives you away!"

Mark looked down at his coat. "Do you like it?" Then he brushed away a tiny piece of fluff from the sleeve. "White is so hard to keep looking sparkling clean though, don't you think?"

Sami peeked out from behind Pradeep's leg and blew a raspberry at Mark.

"Now that's not very polite, young lady," Mark said, looking stern. Then his face softened. "You look so darn cute when you do that I just can't get mad at you. Go on—do it again!"

Sami ducked back to the safety of Pradeep's leg.

"What happened to you, Mark?" I said sitting down at the table with him.

"I don't really remember. I came in and I saw

your lovely cute little goldfish here, and then I suddenly felt all happy and desperately wanted a cup of tea."

Pradeep and I both looked at Frankie.

"Frankie, did you do some kind of hypno-thing to Mark?" I asked.

Sami peeked out and pulled on my pant leg. "Mark not 'swishy fishy,'" she said, doing a pretty good impression of what someone looks like when they've been zombified by Frankie. She should know—she's been zombified enough times herself.

"You're right, Sami," said Pradeep. "He doesn't look as if Frankie's hypnotized him. But then why is he acting so weird and polite?"

"It's like he's gone from being nearly totally evil to being nearly totally nice," I said.

Frankie jumped out of his bucket and flicked a fin. Splashes of greenish water went from his bucket in a straight line to the door. Then he acted out a whole fishy mime that looked

something like a fight scene and involved a lot
of pointing a fin at the door and then at Mark.
I couldn't really get exactly what he meant, but
one thing was clear.

"Has someone else been here, Frankie?" I
asked.

CHAPTER 3

A VERY FISHY PHONE CALL

Frankie fell backward into his bucket with a sigh of relief.

"Who?" Pradeep asked.

Frankie jumped up and yanked Pradeep's sweater with his teeth so that it pulled up over his face.

"Moh, mmmas mmme mmmaring mma maalmeeclava?" Pradeep mumbled from under his sweater.

"Huh?" Sami and I said together.

"Pardon?" Mark echoed.

Pradeep pulled down his sweater as Frankie fell back into the water with a splash. "Oh, was

he wearing a balaclava?" Pradeep repeated. "Was that what you meant, Frankie?"

Frankie nodded.

Pradeep picked up the home phone. "If Mark's not to blame, maybe the levitating-budgie owner might know what's going on. After all, he's the only one apart from us who thinks it's an evil kidnap plot. Now we can add evil brainwashing into the mix."

I held out my arm so Pradeep could read the number from the poster.

Pradeep dialed. The phone rang twice and then a voice answered.

"Password?" it said. It sounded young.

"Sorry?" Pradeep said.

"Passsssswordddd?" it said again, sounding kind of irritated. "On the sign."

Pradeep thought for a moment. "Evil kidnap plot," he said finally.

"OK," the voice said.

"That's technically a 'pass *phrase*,' you

know . . ." Pradeep started to say.

"Do you want me to hang up?" the voice countered.

"No!" I grabbed the phone. "We want to know what happened to the missing pets."

"I'll meet you in the street by my lost-budgie sign in five minutes. How will I know it's you?" the voice answered.

"Well, there'll be me and Pradeep, a toddler dressed as a mermaid, a twelve-year-old in a white Evil Scientist coat . . . oh, and a goldfish in a bucket. I'm pretty sure you'll know it's us," I said. "What do you look like?"

But the voice had already hung up. Or rather, the person with the voice had hung up. Voices don't have hands that can hang up phones.

"Let's go," I said to Pradeep.

"Are we taking Mark with us?" Pradeep asked.

"Well, we can't leave him here for Mom to find," I answered. "She'll think he's got a concussion again and take him to the hospital. He's *never* this nice."

"I really want to help, guys," Mark interrupted. "I can't imagine all those pets out there. Lonely, lost—" he started tearing up—"just wanting a cuddle."

Then he broke down in tears.

"Seriously, do we HAVE to take him?" Pradeep said.

Sami stepped out from behind Pradeep's leg and gave Mark a gentle pat on the back. "There, there," she said.

"Let's just get out there and see what this kid has to say about the missing pets. Maybe he'll know what happened to Mark too," I said, picking up Frankie in the bucket.

Mark wiped his eyes with a hanky. He was actually using a hanky!

Then he looked into the bucket and Frankie growled at him. "Somebody got up on the wrong side of the fishbowl this morning!" sniffed Mark. "You look like you need a hug . . ." and with that he reached into the bucket.

Frankie leaped up and kung fu fish-slapped Mark right across the face!

"Mark, I think that was Frankie's way of saying that he doesn't want a hug," I said, pulling the bucket out of reach. "Now let's go."

We headed out of the door to the lost-levitating-budgie sign, but when we arrived there was nobody there. Pradeep looked closely at the sign. There was an arrow drawn on it, pointing right.

"I'm sure that wasn't there before," he said.

We followed the arrow and it led to a sign for a lost hamster. This one had another arrow drawn on it, pointing straight ahead.

"I think the kid is leading us to him," Pradeep said.

"It's like a treasure hunt. Oh, what fun!" Mark clapped his hands.

Frankie poked his head up out of his bucket and glared. I think the new ultra-nice and polite Mark was getting on his nerves too.

The next arrow led to a sign for a lost gerbil that pointed left, then to a missing snake, which sent us back in a U-turn to where we'd started. Eventually the directions led us to the door of the convenience store.

"It can't be here, can it?" I said.

There was a sign on the door that said: "Only two schoolchildren at a time," so we left Mark and Sami outside playing pat-a-cake. We brought Frankie with us as the sign didn't say

anything about fish and I thought it was safer than leaving him with Mark, just in case Mark tried to hug him again.

When we went inside, Mrs. Martin was standing behind the counter along with a girl sitting on a big stack of newspapers.

The girl looked us up and down and pushed her fringe out of her eyes. "Where's the mermaid and the kid in the white coat?" she demanded.

CHAPTER 4
PETS WITH POWERS

I pointed to the sign about school kids. "Outside," I said. "It's just us and the fish."

"You're the kid with the missing budgie?" Pradeep said. "You're a girl?"

"Nothing gets past you, does it, Sherlock," she replied. "And you're a dweeb, but don't worry, I won't hold it against you if you can help me get my budgie back."

"I didn't mean . . ." Pradeep stuttered and suddenly found something on the floor that he had to look at for a long time.

"Sorry," the girl said. "I'm just worried about Boris."

We must have both given her a look that said, "Who?" because she said, "My budgie. Come on— try to keep up, people!"

"We want to help," I said. "I'm Tom and this is Pradeep."

The girl raised an eyebrow. "My hacker handle is Geeky Girl," she said. "Better you don't know my real name."

She jumped down off the stack of papers and shouted to Mrs. Martin, "I'm just gonna hang with my friends for a bit, OK, Mom?" Then she motioned for us to come through the doorway to the back of the shop. "Better bring the others too. I've got something to show you all."

We brought in Mark and Sami and, after Mark had complimented Mrs. Martin on her new hairstyle, discussed the weather and reached up to a high shelf to get down some cans of beans she needed, we headed into the apartment behind the shop.

"Welcome to Lost Pet HQ," Geeky Girl said as

she brought us into her room. It was absolutely *full* of computer stuff. Pradeep was looking around like a kid in candy land.

There were keyboards, screens, cameras and wires. A lot of wires. There were also pictures up on the walls of all the missing pets and pieces of string connecting them all like a giant pet web.

"Wow, it's like one of those boards they have on TV crime shows," I said.

"It's my incident board for missing pets." She smiled. "And I've done a lot of research online too."

Pradeep was sitting at one of her laptops now, scrolling through pictures. "I was on this website earlier," he said. "Lots of pets are missing in a very concentrated area."

"Exactly. They're all from in and around this neighborhood," she said, "but there's a more obvious connection. All the missing pets have special powers."

"What?" we all said at the same time.

Then Mark said, "Oh, sorry to talk over you. You first!"

"The pets that have been kidnapped had all been named online by their owners as having powers." She tapped away at another keyboard and pictures came up on a big screen, with names and descriptions underneath.

"Toby telepopping tortoise!" Sami said, pointing to a picture of Toby.

FLUFFY
Psychic bunny

MOLLY
Nearly invisible poodle

HENRY
Time-travelling hamster

TOBY
Teleporting tortoise

Pradeep and I saw the girl's look and both said at once, "Teleporting tortoise!"

"That's from the website. Someone must have posted something about the tortoise's power," she said.

"I think my cousin put something about it on his SmileBook page," Pradeep said.

"It's all connected," she said darkly.

Another picture came up on the screen. This one showed a serious-looking green-and-yellow budgie.

"That's Boris, my levitating budgie," she said.

"Doesn't that just mean he can fly?" Pradeep said "I mean, he *is* a bird."

Geeky Girl glared at Pradeep in the same way that Frankie had been glaring at Mark.

"So all these pets are supposedly *super*-pets?" I said. "That's even stranger. Why kidnap a bunch of mildly super pets?"

"I don't know," she said. "I haven't figured that bit out yet. I was hoping that *you* guys

would have some information."

"Well, my brother Mark, who is usually incredibly evil, has been turned incredibly nice," I replied. "I don't know if that's related."

"If there's one thing that you learn from reading all the papers every day, it's that nothing happens by chance," she said.

"There's one more thing that we should probably tell you about too," I went on. "There's *definitely* something special about our goldfish."

CHAPTER 5
ZOMBIE HIDE-AND-SEEK

"Have you posted anything online about him?"
Geeky Girl asked, frowning.

Pradeep and I looked at each other. "No," we
both said at the same time.

"What does he do?" she said, staring at Frankie
who was just in normal goldfish mode now,
doing laps of backstroke in his bucket. Well,
normal for Frankie, anyway.

"Can he fly? Turn invisible? Walk through
walls? Shrink? Grow? Go super-stretchy? Jump
into alternative dimensions? Bend space?" She
paused and looked at us. "I read a lot of comics,"
she added. "So what's the deal?"

"It's hard to describe," Pradeep said.

"Swishy fishy zombie fishy," Sami interrupted. "Swirly, swirly eyes!" Then she started walking around doing her best zombie goldfish impression.

We looked at Geeky Girl, waiting for a response to the fact that we had just admitted to owning a zombie goldfish.

"Cool," with a vague nod, was the only reaction we got.

"It's good you've kept it off the Internet," she added. "That's just the kind of pet that would attract the attention of the kidnapper."

"We were so sure the kidnapper was Mark," I said. "Whenever there's an evil plot, he's usually behind it."

"Him?" Geeky Girl stared at Mark in disbelief.

Then Pradeep spoke up, "What if Sanj is involved?"

"Who's Sanj?" said Geeky Girl.

"My Evil Computer Genius big brother," Pradeep replied.

"You two have weird families," Geeky Girl said with a frown.

"But Sanj is away at boarding school, right?" I said.

"Yes, and Mom and Dad even had a Skype call with him yesterday. He was definitely in his room at school. There's no way he could have kidnapped any pets around here today or earlier this week," Pradeep said.

"If it's not him," Geeky Girl said, pacing the floor, "then we have to track down the real kidnapper, and fast."

"Find Toby," Sami sniffled.

"I say, you're all looking rather stressed again. Why don't I go and ask that charming Mrs.

Martin if I can make you all some camomile tea? I know I could certainly use a cup!" Mark said, standing up.

"There will be NO TEA until we get Boris back," Geeky Girl yelled, slamming the table with her fist.

"That's a little extreme, don't you think?" Mark whispered to me.

"Extreme!" I said out loud. "That's it. We need to think extreme." I looked around at their confused faces. "If the kidnapper wants to find special pets, then we have to let him think he's found an *extremely* special one."

Pradeep stood up. "Yes, let's post something up on the Internet about a super-special pet and see if the kidnapper will strike. Then we can catch him in the act!"

"The problem is," I said slowly, "the only special pet we have is Frankie, and we don't want to risk posting anything online about his *actual* powers."

Frankie jumped out of his bucket and splashed us.

"Not now, Frankie," Pradeep said.

But Frankie jumped out again anyway. This time he landed on Mark's head, nibbled off a lock of hair and jumped back into the bucket.

"I say, little fish, that's extremely rude!" Mark looked at his hair in the reflection of one of the computer screens. "I have to admit though, it did need a trim and you've done a great job . . ."

"Frankie, what are you doing?" I said.

Frankie jumped up again and this time snatched Pradeep's glasses from his nose with a single swipe.

"Hey!" cried Pradeep. "I need those!"

Frankie splashed back into the bucket and peered up at us with the glasses on his face and the lock of hair above his mouth like a fishy mustache.

"Aha!" I said. "You're in disguise!"

"If we disguise Frankie as some other kind of super-creature, then we won't  risk anyone finding out he's actually a zombie goldfish," Pradeep said.

"Good thinking, Frankie," I said. "But I still don't like the idea of using you as bait to catch the kidnapper."

Frankie jumped up and the mustache and glasses went flying as he fishy-karate-chopped the air.

"I know, you can take care of yourself," I huffed as I leaped to catch Pradeep's glasses. "But we'll be right there too as backup."

Frankie plopped back into the bucket as I handed Pradeep his soggy glasses.

"So, what shall we disguise your goldfish as?"
Geeky Girl asked.

We thought about that.

"How could anyone want to kidnap this cute
little fishy?" Mark said, leaning over the bucket
and reaching out his hand to stroke Frankie.

In a second Frankie went into zombie green-
eyed attack mode and snapped at Mark's fingers.

"That fish is more like a piranha than a goldfish," said Geeky Girl, sounding far more impressed now than when we first revealed that Frankie was a zombie goldfish.

Then Pradeep got what could only be described as a giant lightbulb over his head. "Then that's what he'll be! We've got some green paint left and we can make a bigger tail and body with tinfoil. He'll look great." He started typing away on one of the keyboards and a picture of an Amazonian piranha came up on screen. "We could totally make Frankie look like that."

"Then we'll just have to put a photo and some posts on the net about our super-poisonous pinching piranha," Geeky Girl added. "It'll be a challenge the kidnapper won't be able to resist."

CHAPTER 6
FISHY FOUL PLAY

Sami and I set to work on the transformation of Frankie while Pradeep and Geeky Girl set up some hidden cameras with microphones in the living room. Luckily Mrs. Martin had a fish tank in the shop that we could use to put Frankie in. Man, that corner shop has *everything*!

"Fishy stay still!" Sami said as Frankie thrashed away while she was trying to stick on the tinfoil tail.

"Come on, Frankie. It was your idea to be in disguise," I whispered to him.

Frankie flopped over on his back with a fishy sigh and stayed still so Sami could do the tail sticking.

Then I touched up the green paint around his gills and mouth.

Mark spent his time helpfully opening doors, handing us bits of stuff we needed and bringing us all endless cups of tea. I mean, we're kids. We don't really drink tea! This new, nice, helpful Mark was really freaking me out.

When Frankie was ready, Sami went and got a mirror from Geeky Girl's nightstand.

"Fishy look scary!" Sami said with a smile. "Snap, snap, snap fishy teeth."

We angled the mirror so Frankie could see himself. As soon as he caught a glimpse he went into immediate zombie attack stance, ready to fight whatever creature was about to attack him. Until he realized he was looking at himself!

"So what do you think, Frankie?" I said.

"You look like a very poisonous pinching piranha to me," Mark said.

Frankie glared at his reflection, then struck a couple of action poses.

"I think he approves." I grinned.

When Pradeep and Geeky Girl were done with all the technical stuff we took a photo of Frankie, uploaded it to the web and waited. Almost as soon as we had put it online, Mark's phone rang. We all jumped.

"Hello, Mom!" Mark beamed down the phone. "Yes, Tom and Pradeep and Sami are all with me. We're having a lovely time dressing up the fish . . ." I grabbed the phone off Mark.

"Hi, Mom, it's Tom."

"Are you boys OK? You don't normally hang out with Mark unless I make you," she said.

"Really, we're fine, we went to the shops and then had a nice cup of tea," I said. As soon as the words left my mouth, I could picture the face Mom was making. No way would she believe me!

"OK . . ." She paused. "And what's all this about dressing up the fish?"

"Oh, Sami's in her mermaid outfit. Mark was

just making a joke. She's dressed as a fish, get it?"
I tried.

"No, but never mind. I'll be home in a few
hours. Just head over to Pradeep's house when
you're done and I'll pick you up from there. I'll
let his mom know that her kids are with Mark
too and you'll head over soon."

We just had time to breathe before the computer
beeped. Geeky Girl had set up the website to alert
us when anyone viewed the picture.

"So we know someone has spotted it. If they're
the kidnapper, then we've got to be ready,"
Pradeep had said.

Geeky Girl, Mark and Sami all stayed in Lost
Pet HQ while Pradeep and I carried Frankie
in the fish tank into the living room. All the
cameras were trained on the tank.

Pradeep and I hid. We were ready to jump out
as soon as anything suspicious happened.

Half an hour slid slowly by, then an hour.
The thing they don't tell you about stakeouts on

spy shows is that they are really, *really*, REALLY boring. Pradeep went through maths problems in his head to make himself stay awake. I tried the same technique, but was asleep by 2 x ZZZzzzzzz. I was jolted awake by a crash outside the room.

Something or someone was in the hall. Pradeep and I gave each other our look that meant, "This is it!"

We both jumped out from our hiding places and ran into the hall. There was a window open and the table beneath it had pieces of a broken vase lying around it. Someone must have climbed through the window and broken the vase getting in! As we were looking at the broken china on the floor we heard the living-room door slam behind us and the lock click. We ran back to the door and rattled the handle. We were locked out!

The kidnapper must be inside, and so was Frankie!

CHAPTER 7

THE KIDNAPPER STRIKES

"We know you're in there . . . pet-kidnapper person!" I shouted.

"Yeah, and you're trapped so you might as well give yourself up now," Pradeep added.

We rattled the doorknob and pushed on the door again, but it wouldn't budge. We could hear crashing about from inside the room.

"Frankie!" I shouted.

"Maybe we can get in through the living-room window," Pradeep yelled, already running down the hall, "if we go around the side of the building. Come on!"

As we raced past Geeky Girl's room we

shouted, "The kidnapper's got Frankie. Come on!"

We ran out of the front of the shop, past Mrs. Martin, who was selling a customer a paper, and around the side of the building. As Pradeep hoisted me up so I could look into the window, we heard the living-room door slam again.

"Maybe that's Mark and Geeky Girl," I said. "Maybe they broke down the door."

But when I looked in the window the room was empty. No kidnapper, no Mark, no Geeky Girl.

But worse, no, much, *much* worse . . . no Frankie!

We heard a startled squeal from Mrs. Martin and raced back to the shop.

"What happened?"

Pradeep and I asked Mrs. Martin together.

"He scared the life out of me," she said, fanning herself with a newspaper. "He just ran out through the shop. He was carrying a bag. Oh my, have we been robbed?" She sat down on the pile of newspapers.

"No!" Pradeep and I said at the same time.

I had to think quickly. There was no way we could tell Mrs. Martin that our zombie goldfish, disguised as a poisonous pinching piranha, had been kidnapped as part of an evil plot to kidnap paranormal pets!

"I mean," I began, "it's, er, a game we're playing. You know . . . the guy with the bag is 'It,' and we have to chase him!"

"Well, you were making a terrible racket!" The color seemed to come back to Mrs. Martin's cheeks. "I was just about to yell up to tell you to stop crashing around in there when that boy ran out," she said.

"A boy?" I said.

"Yes," she said, standing up. "In a black hood thing. I suppose part of your game too? Now can you all just play quietly for a while?"

"Yes, Mrs. Martin," we said together, and raced back to Geeky Girl's bedroom.

Pradeep shot me a look that said, "Phew, at least Mrs. Martin bought our story!"

"But where are Geeky Girl and Mark?" I said out loud. "Why didn't they try to stop the kidnapper when we called them?"

We opened the door to find Geeky Girl asking Mark if he fancied a nice cup of tea. Sami was chanting "Swishy little fishy!" quietly to herself with her fingers in her ears as she stared at one of the computer screens with one eye and up Mark's left nostril with the other.

Mark pulled his earphones out of his ears. "Pardon? What did you say?" he said to Geeky Girl. "I've just been listening to some whale song to relax. You really should try it."

Geeky Girl turned to Pradeep and me. "You

both look quite upset. I was just saying that
a cup of tea would be lovely," she said with a
winning smile.

"It's happened to her too," Pradeep cried.

"Noooo! She's been nicified!" I croaked.

We bolted back to the living room to look for
clues. There were blobs of green paint and torn
bits of foil floating in the tank and strewn all
around the room.

"Whatever happened, Frankie didn't go easily,"
Pradeep said.

"And most of the disguise has come off, so the
kidnapper must have known he wasn't getting
a poisonous pinching piranha, but he took him
anyway," I said.

"I just hope the cameras caught something, or
we'll be no closer to knowing who the kidnapper
is. We'll have lost Frankie for nothing!" Pradeep
exclaimed.

We headed back to the Lost Pet HQ, aka
Geeky Girl's bedroom. Geeky Girl and Mark were

happily drinking tea, while Sami had wandered over to the incident board of missing-pet photos and had her back to us. She still had her fingers in her ears.

Pradeep pulled up the video feed from the cameras. You could see the door opening and closing and then see it shaking. "That must be us trying to get in," I said. "But why can't we see who's in there with Frankie?"

The cameras were focused on the tank and the door in the background. Then we saw a figure come into view from the last place we expected . . . the ceiling! A hooded figure dropped down on a wire and hung suspended

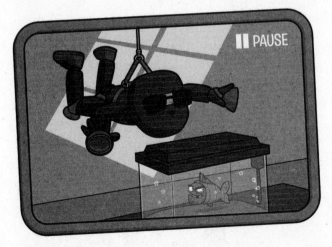

over the tank, *Mission: Impossible*-style. We
paused the video.

"Now, that is cool," Pradeep and I said at the
same time. "Evil, but cool."

CHAPTER 8

A ZOMBIE CONNECTION

"Look—he's got sucker cups on his hands and knees!" cried Pradeep, rewinding the video and playing it again at half-speed. "He must have come in through the window and hidden on the hall ceiling, and then crawled into the living room when we were distracted by the broken vase on the floor."

Next the video showed Frankie jumping up and starting to fish-slap the kidnapper as he hung from the ceiling like a giant spider. You could tell Frankie was trying to zombie stare him too, but the guy was wearing tinted glasses and a balaclava. Lots of the tinfoil came off Frankie

in the fight. The kidnapper grabbed at Frankie several times before he finally caught him in a gloved hand. Then with the other hand he grabbed what looked like a ray gun of some kind. Not that I've seen a lot of ray guns, but this is kind of what I would imagine a ray gun to look like—all metal, with lights on the side and a cone-like thing at the front that sort of looked like a showerhead. Suddenly Frankie lurched toward one of the cameras and stared directly at the lens.

"Quick, look away!" I shouted at Pradeep, covering his eyes and closing mine. "He's doing the zombie stare."

"Swishy fishy. Must find swishy fishy." I looked

over to see Sami still staring up at the incident board with her ears plugged.

"Oh great! Now that's set her off," Pradeep said.

"Um . . . Pradeep, I think she's actually hypnotized!" I said, remembering that Sami had been staring at the computer screens when we first came into the room. "She must have been looking at the screen when Frankie stared into the camera!"

Then we heard a splash and looked back at the video screens. Frankie was now in a dark bag. The kidnapper held up his ray gun to the camera microphone and pressed a button.
A flash went off and then a click and a high "Hummmmmmm . . ." noise. Pradeep quickly leaned across and turned off the volume button.

"That sound," he said. "It's barely in the audible range for humans. Only kids would be able to hear it."

"How do you know that?" I said, shaking my

head to try to get rid of the ringing in my ears. "Ouch, that hurts."

"I did a project on the frequency of sound waves last year," Pradeep said. "As you grow up you lose the ability to hear really high-pitched sounds. I think that *that* sound must have something to do with Mark and Geeky Girl turning so horribly nice."

"But why would the kidnapper use a frequency that only affects kids?" I asked.

"It was the kids who posted the information online about their super-pets. Maybe the pet kidnapper thought if he turned the pet owners 'mostly nice,' they wouldn't stop him from taking their pets."

"So why would they put up Missing signs then?" I asked.

"The kidnapper would expect that if the kids' parents wanted to put up signs, the kids would be too polite not to help! It's evil, but clever!"

"But why was Mark affected? He doesn't have

a pet to steal!" I went on. "And why was Geeky Girl nicified, but Mark wasn't double-nicified . . . or un-nicified? And what about Sami? Is she nice-zombified?" I stopped as I was confusing myself with my made-up words.

"You boys really ought to listen to this whale song. It's *soooo* soothing," Mark said, holding his earphones out toward Geeky Girl.

"Wait! Mark was listening to that clicking, whining, whale stuff when the ray gun went off. And Sami was already zombified! Frankie must have made her put her fingers in her ears, so that's why only Geeky Girl actually heard it," Pradeep said.

"A spot of whale song sounds lovely," Geeky Girl said. "May I?" She reached for the earphones.

I rolled my eyes. "I don't think I can take *both* of them being like this."

"So now we're stuck with two nicified people and one zombified toddler, and we're no closer to finding out who the kidnapper is or finding

Frankie," Pradeep said, slumping into a chair.

At that moment, Sami took her fingers out of her ears and wandered toward the door. "Must find swishy fishy," she mumbled.

"Do you think," I said to Pradeep, "that Sami could somehow be zombie-linked to Frankie? Maybe she can help us find him."

Pradeep jumped up. "That's brilliant! Frankie must have hypnotized Sami to create a zombie psychic connection! All we need to do now is let

Sami lead us to him before the kidnapper does something that will break the connection."

"But the only way that could happen is if Frankie gets knocked out or . . ." I stopped. I didn't want to think about what else would break the link.

CHAPTER 9
EVIL BROTHERS "R" US

We said good-bye to Mrs. Martin as we left the shop.

"Mother, you are looking lovely today," Geeky Girl said as she held the door open for Sami.

We practically had to drag Mark away from his conversation with Mrs. Martin about how gardens really do need a little rain at this time of the year. I was very worried. I mean, not that it wasn't great not to have Mark threatening to pummel me every few minutes. But seriously, what if he was stuck this way forever? I thought about living with the new, polite version of Mark—not wedging me in the dog flap of

the kitchen door, not loosening the wheels of
my skateboard, not randomly plotting world
domination. It seemed nice, but also kind of boring.

We headed down the road, closely following
Sami.

"After you," Mark said, standing aside to let
Geeky Girl go first.

"No, no, after you." She smiled.

"Really, I insist," he said.

"Oh, just one of you go first! Sami is toddling
away!" I shouted.

Sami mumbled "Swishy little fishy" to herself as she toddled through the park and out the other side. She turned left at the next street. As we approached the next turning Pradeep said sadly, "She's not taking us to Frankie. We were wrong, Tom. She's just heading home."

Sure enough, Pradeep's house was on the next road, right next to mine. Sami walked across her front lawn and then started heading around the side of the house.

"So Frankie wasn't leading us to him after all." I kicked the fence with my sneaker. "Now how are we going to find him?"

"Wait," Pradeep said. "She's heading around the back toward the garage. If she was heading home, she'd just go to the front door, right? So maybe she *is* leading us to Frankie after all."

"If it's your house, and the kidnapper is there, do you think it could be . . ." I started, and Pradeep finished my thought: "Sanj?"

We decided to go into stealth mode to

sneak around the back of the house.

But it's kind of hard being in stealth mode with a toddler who keeps saying "Swishy little fishy" and the politeness twins.

"Here, let me hold that branch out of your way, I insist."

"Please, let me open that gate for you."

We managed to shut them up for long enough to listen at the back door of the garage. We could hear classical music playing inside.

"Well, somebody's in there," I said.

"And that somebody doesn't want anyone out here to hear any unusual noises from in there. They're masking any strange sounds with music!" Pradeep replied.

"Like the sound of all the missing pets!" we said together and high-fived. It was a kind of high-five moment.

"All those poor lost pets," Mark snuffled.

"Boris and the others must be so scared," Geeky Girl added, tears welling up in her eyes.

Pradeep grabbed a pack of tissues from his back pocket. "I always have some on me for hay fever emergencies," he explained. He passed them back to Geeky Girl and Mark.

"Thank you. You're too kind," they sniffled.

We had to get inside somehow, but just barging in didn't really fit in with the stealth plan.

"Next to the garage is a vent that leads out of the laundry room. I could fit through it with Sami. Then if she still tries to head into the garage, we'll know Frankie's in there," Pradeep said.

"Or you could just use your front-door key?" I whispered.

"Oh yes," said Pradeep sheepishly. "Or that."

"I'll wait here with these two and you can open the laundry-room door from the inside," I said.

We waited a minute and then heard the latch turn on the laundry-room door. We tiptoed in, following Pradeep, who was still following Sami.

It was only then that I fully realized that we didn't have an *actual* plan of what to do once we got inside.

As soon as we opened the back door of the garage we were hit by a wall of sound. Every kind of quack, hiss, chirp, screech, growl, miaow, woof and stomp that an animal could make was coming from in there! The classical music boomed over the top of it all, and sitting with his back to us in a desk chair in front of a computer was Sanj, air-conducting the music.

I put my finger to my lips and looked at Mark and Geeky Girl.

"Shouldn't we ask if it's all right to come in?" Geeky Girl whispered.

"We don't want to be rude," Mark added.

I rolled my eyes and mouthed, "Shhhhh!"

Pradeep and I silently pushed the door wider and we all stepped into the room.

Now, I don't know how many times Pradeep, Sami and I have been caught in the last year in a booby trap, but whatever the total was, we were just about to add one more.

In our defense, there was no way we could have expected a booby trap like this. This booby trap involved an actual booby!

CHAPTER 10
NEVER TRUST A BOOBY

As soon as we were through the door, a big white bird with blue feet (which I later found out was a blue-footed booby) squawked, then nudged a bowling ball that was at the top of a ramp. The ball rolled down the slope and tipped a scale that sent a tennis racket swinging above our heads. The racket thwacked a lever that started a turntable that swung a fishing rod that held a net above our heads. When after a couple of seconds the net didn't drop I heard a voice say, "Oh for goodness sake! Bird!"

Then the bird flew off its perch and pecked at the net, which dropped neatly onto our heads.

That all actually happened in much less time than it took to explain it.

As the blue-footed booby cleaned its feathers, I looked at the bird. One of its eyes was looking at the wall and the other was looking up my left nostril. It had the zombie stare!

This was not good. We had fallen for the ultimate booby trap and now we were, well . . . trapped.

The classical music finished and Sanj slowly

swiveled his desk chair around.

"Perfect timing," he said. "I see you like my booby trap!" He giggled to himself with his normal wheezy laugh that just never sounded quite evil enough. "I found the blue-footed booby in a bird sanctuary. They said it could tap dance, but its sense of rhythm is appalling."

Mark spoke first. "Lovely to see you, Sanj." He motioned to Geeky Girl, "Let me introduce . . . Oh, I'm dreadfully sorry—I don't know your real name?"

"It's Glenda," said Geeky Girl. No wonder she didn't want to tell us her name before! "I'm so pleased to meet you." She tried to hold out her hand, but it was trapped under the net so she just nodded and smiled.

"Mark, it hurts me to see a fellow evil-doer reduced to . . . *this*, but I had to do it," Sanj said, shaking his head.

"So you did do this to Mark?" I said.

"And it has something to do with that sound

frequency you used at . . ." Pradeep paused. "Glenda's house."

"Mark was collateral damage." Sanj shrugged. "We went to your house, Tom, to get that goldfish *again*. The plan was to trap Frankie alive so that we could harness his hypnotic energy to help us to control an evil army of zombified super-pets." Sanj smiled. "I had already accumulated the army. It was so *easy* once I used the Supersonic Nicifying Helpful Minion Ray on the children who owned the pets—they couldn't have been more helpful. They handed over their pets quite

 happily. Some of them even gave me cupcakes or brownies just to be extra nice. It was sweet. Pathetic, but sweet." Sanj did his evil wheeze. "By

the time I had left with their pets, they couldn't remember a thing that had happened. It's a very convenient side effect of the ray. Short-term memory loss . . ."

"But you—" I started to say.

"It's not polite to interrupt an Evil Computer Genius when he's explaining his overly complicated evil plot, Tom. Where are your manners?" Mark said.

I really couldn't take much more of this Mark.

"But Mark changed his mind when we got to your house. He said that these plans never end up with him ever being able to actually splat the fish, which is all he really wants to do, so this time he was going to *start* the plan by splatting the fish while he had the chance." Sanj took a breath. "So you see, I had to use the Supersonic Nicifying Helpful Minon Ray on him. Unfortunately I got the dosage a bit wrong and . . . well, you can see the result. Then you all came back in and I had to make a quick

getaway—unfortunately without the fish."

Sami, who had somehow avoided the booby-trap netting, was standing in front of a fish tank with Frankie inside. "Swishy fishy sad," she mumbled.

Frankie had a little harness around his middle and had cameras pointed at his eyes and little earphones over his head.

"You know goldfish don't have ears, right?" Pradeep said.

"Of course." Sanj glared at Pradeep. "But they hear through a stone in their heads. I can send the sound waves to that stone. That way Frankie can hypnotize all the other animals and I can make Frankie nice and polite with my Supersonic Nicifying Helpful Minion Ray so he'll do whatever I ask."

CHAPTER 11
ZOMBIE MINIONS

I pictured a nice, well-mannered Frankie who would do anything that Sanj wanted. It was awful!

"The hypnotizing of the blue-footed booby went perfectly, so we're just about ready to begin with all the other animals." Sanj grinned. "What a perfect time to arrive!"

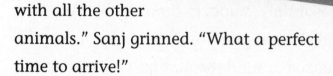

We had to get Frankie out of there now, before it was too late.

I shot Pradeep a look that said, "I'm going to try to get free and rescue Frankie; you keep Sanj talking."

Pradeep nodded. "It's a very clever plan, Sanj," he said, wearing his best "I'm being polite and interested" face that he uses at school. "Do tell me more."

"At first I thought that if I researched on the Internet long enough I could find a pet with super-powers that could be the arch-nemesis of that annoying goldfish, so we could defeat him once and for all. So I snuck out of boarding school and set up this lair in the garage with one corner that looks like my room at school, so I could fool Mom and Dad into thinking I was still there, and also virtually attend my lectures. I didn't want my grades to drop just because I'm busy with an evil plan this week."

We looked around the garage. One corner

had been set up with a bed and a desk and posters of other Evil Computer Geniuses on the wall. I maneuverd myself behind Pradeep and wriggled one of my legs free.

"But didn't the teachers wonder why you didn't show up for class?" Pradeep said.

"I sent an e-mail from the Institute of Highly Contagious Diseases that said I had a rare virus and needed to be quarantined in my room, but I'd be set up with a webcam." He smirked.

"And your mom and dad didn't notice that you were sneaking animals into their garage and playing loud classical music?" I asked.

"We had the garage mostly soundproofed when I told my parents that I wanted to learn the drums last summer. I just knew that it would come in handy to have a soundproof lair."

"And I love what you've done with it!" added Mark.

"Thank you." Sanj smiled. "We talked on Skype a couple of times this week. They could see my . . . 'room' . . . so had no reason to suspect that I wasn't at school."

My other leg was now free too. If Pradeep could just keep Sanj talking for a little longer then maybe I could get to Frankie, grab him and run. My plan hadn't got any further than that.

"Go on," said Pradeep encouragingly.

"But none of the pets were strong enough or had any really useful special powers. Take this one—" Sanj tapped a cage, and a pair of pink bows and a collar appeared at the door. If you squinted, you could make out a very, very, *very* pale-beige, bored-looking poodle standing there wearing the bows and collar. "A nearly invisible poodle—what good is that?" Sanj huffed. He walked over to a cage containing a brown rabbit who sat with a deck of cards under its back paws. "Red Queen," Sanj mumbled and the rabbit thumped the back of one of the cards. Sanj pulled out the card from the cage and it was the Queen of Hearts. "A psychic rabbit!

Hardly going to strike fear, is it?" He shook his head and walked back to Frankie's tank. "But a whole army of paranormal pets together—now that could be fun. Now, please excuse me while I make Frankie zombify the other animals. Then all that's left to do is to zap him with the Supersonic Nicifying Helpful Minion Ray to put him completely under my control."

"Oh, don't mind us trapped under the net here. You look very busy with your evil plan. We can wait," Mark said, and Geeky Girl nodded.

"Wakey, wakey, everyone." Sanj banged on the cages and tanks. Each of the cages was fitted with a screen that showed a close-up shot of Frankie's eyes.

All the animals woke up except for a tiny kitten in the corner of her cage. Sanj rattled the cage and the kitten mewed at him, glanced over and then curled up facing away from the door.

"Oh no, you're getting zombified too, little kitty. Wake up." Sanj opened the door and reached into the cage to shake the kitten awake. As soon as his hand entered the cage the kitten leaped at it and sunk its teeth into Sanj's thumb.

"Argh!" he cried out. "Stupid moron cat!" He slammed the cage door shut and wrapped some tissues around his bleeding hand.

"That one was called a 'vampire kitten' on the pet-forum website. I should have left it in solitary confinement at the cats' home where I found it."

"Oh, the poor little thing is probably just scared and needs a cuddle. Don't you, kitty-witty?" Mark said.

The kitten glanced over at Mark, then sharpened its very pointy teeth on the bars of its cage.

Sanj went over and stood by Frankie's tank in the middle of the room. He looked down at Sami, who was still staring into the tank mumbling, "Swishy fishy sad."

"It's no good hypnotizing my little sister again, fish. She can't help you! Not when I'll soon have an army of zombie pets under my control." Then he let out a feeble "Mwhaaa . . . haaa . . . haaa . . . haaa!"

CHAPTER 12

PARANORMAL PLANS

Even ultra-polite Mark couldn't *not* say
something. "That's an A for effort, Sanj, but you
really need more diaphragm support when you
do your evil laugh. But I'm sure with a bit of
practice it'll be just fine."

Sanj scowled. "I definitely preferred you as
mostly evil." Then he flipped the switch and
the cameras in front of Frankie's eyes turned on.
Frankie thrashed his head from side to side as if
he was trying to resist looking at the cameras,
but the harness held him in place.

"Don't look, Frankie!" I shouted. "Don't do it."

"Excuse me for interrupting," Mark said, "but

the fish needs to be way angrier to do his zombie stare."

"Thanks for the reminder." Sanj smirked.

"Mark!" Pradeep and I yelled.

"It was only polite to tell him," Geeky Girl said.

"Thank you for your support, Glenda," Mark replied.

"Shut up!" Sanj shouted at Mark and Geeky Girl. "Are they like this all the time?" he said to us.

We nodded.

"Right, now . . . how to make Frankie angry . . ."

"Stay calm, Frankie, stay calm," I muttered. My escape-from-the-net plan was not going well. My legs were free, but unfortunately, none of the rest of me.

"Maybe I should try the sonic ray on Sami," Sanj said, leaning toward Frankie's tank. "It would be cute to have a toddler at the front of my zombie pet army."

"No!" yelled Pradeep. "Sanj, I'm going to tell Mom on you!"

"Mom's not here." Sanj grinned, pointing the ray at Sami's head.

Frankie's eyes glowed green with rage until they looked as if they were going to pop out of his head.

Sanj laughed his normal wheezy laugh. "To quote the mostly evil version of you, Mark, 'Result!'"

Images of Frankie's zombie stare appeared on every screen in every animal cage.

The woofs, quacks and screeches that had filled the garage suddenly fell silent. I looked around. All the animals in their cages and tanks had the same zombie stare. They were all under Frankie's control! Maybe if I could release them before Frankie got zapped with the Supersonic Nicifying Helpful Minion Ray we could still all escape. Trying not to attract Sanj's attention, I carried on wriggling the rest of my body out from under the net.

"It would have been so much simpler if I could have just nicified the fish first, but it's very hard to make a super-helpful nicified fish annoyed." Sanj shook his head as he strolled back to his desk and started fiddling with his computer.

Something bumped into my foot. It was Toby! The tortoise stood by my sneaker, staring at the wall with one eye and up at the blue-footed booby's beak with the other. I noticed that Sami was now standing by Toby's cage, silently closing the door.

"Now all I need to do is turn the fish nice and polite with my Supersonic Nicifying Helpful Minion Ray and he'll tell my pet army to do whatever I want," Sanj wheezed. He checked each of the cages and tanks to see that the zombie stare had worked. When he got to the kitten he stopped and put on an oven glove before reaching into the cage. The kitten sprang as soon as the door was open and sunk her teeth into Sanj's gloved hand.

"I guess the vampire kitten slept through the zombie stare," Pradeep said.

"No matter. What good can a kitten do in a zombie army anyway?" Sanj grabbed the kitten by the scruff of her neck, removed the oven glove and shoved her into it. Then he taped the glove tight around her so just her head was sticking out. "I'll return you to the cats' home later," he snarled, dropping her on the floor next to Frankie's tank.

"Now see here," Mark said, standing slightly

taller, even though he was still trapped in a net. "That's no way to treat a kitten, vampire or not."

"I don't have time for this," Sanj snapped. "I have an evil plan to implement." He turned around and started typing away on a keyboard. "I'll have to charge the Supersonic Nicifying Helpful Minion Ray to maximum if this is going to work."

Then I noticed Sami had moved again. She was back at Frankie's tank, slipping Toby the tortoise into the water. Darn, that tortoise was fast! He'd been standing by my sneaker only a second ago.

Sanj had his back to us and was connecting some kind of wires to the ray gun. "For maximum control, I'll be sending the sound waves directly to the earphones on the fish," he muttered.

"Tom, you have to move now!" Pradeep whispered. "As soon as Sanj turns on the ray gun, it'll be too late! Frankie will do whatever Sanj wants just to be polite. And the other animals under Frankie's power will do whatever Sanj wants too. He's going to get his paranormal pet army!"

CHAPTER 13
TO ZAP A ZOMBIE

"There!" Sanj adjusted another dial on the ray gun. "Charged to maximum. We're ready to begin." He flicked the switch and the gun vibrated on the table.

Toby, still not noticed by Sanj, had sunk to the bottom of Frankie's tank. He crawled over to the wire that ran from the ray gun to Frankie's earphones and in one mighty chomp he broke the connection. But had he done it in time?

Sanj looked at his computer screen and then started fiddling with buttons on the keyboard. "The readings are wrong," he muttered. "It should have worked by now." Then he put on some

CHOMP!

ear protectors and grabbed the ray gun, pulling
out the wires. He stood up. "I'll have to do it the
old-fashioned way," he said, heading for the
tank. Looking over at us he said, "At maximum
setting, it's guaranteed to affect you all as well,
but it will be lovely to have you all as my
helpful nicified minions. I'm sure you'll all come
in very . . . useful!"

By now I was completely out of the net
and ready to jump on Sanj as soon as he got
close enough. I could also see that Toby had
chomped through the harness that held

Frankie to the floor of the tank.

"How did you get . . . ?" said Sanj in surprise, leaning over the tank and looking at Toby. Before he could finish his sentence, Frankie jumped out of the tank and fish-slapped Sanj across the face with his tail. Sanj dropped the ray gun and fell backward. I leaped forward, arms out to grab the ray gun, but somehow I slipped and ended up on the floor face-to-face with the vampire kitten, which bit me on the nose.

"Ow!" I yelled, trying to pull the kitten off my face as Sanj picked up the ray gun and Frankie flip-flopped on the floor.

Sami scooped Toby out of the tank and stood beside me mumbling, "Swishy fishy."

"Frankie, please stop," Sanj said quietly.

Frankie stopped flip-flopping and turned toward Sanj. It was as if he couldn't help himself. He was too polite to disobey.

"Thank you, Frankie," Sanj said.

"No!" I gasped.

"Some of the Supersonic Nicifying Helpful Minion Rays must have got through to him on the earphones before that stupid tortoise bit through the wire! It only takes a second to work. Now, fish, go and pop yourself into that glass of water on the desk. You're no good to me if you're a fish out of water." Sanj laughed at his own joke and Frankie obeyed immediately. Then Sanj spoke again. "Frankie, could you please make all the animals pay attention so that I can tell you what I would like them to do? And, Tom, don't even think about moving, or I'll use the ray gun on all of you."

Frankie glared but then nodded. Suddenly all the zombified animals were all looking over at Sanj.

"Frankie, please fight it!" I cried.

"He can't." Sanj laughed. "That wouldn't be *nice* now, would it?"

Mark chimed in. "He is right about that, Tom."

"It would be terribly rude. Especially as he's a guest," Geeky Girl agreed.

Sami mumbled, "Swishy fishy no!"

"Now, I would like all of my new-found animal army to assemble on the driveway. We are going to march into town and take over the radio station. Then we can release the Supersonic Nicifying Helpful Minion Ray onto the airwaves and every kid who hears it will become my helpful minion and do whatever I want. My first step toward world domination. Once again."

Sanj opened all the cages and upturned the tanks. All the

animals slithered, crawled or skittered toward the garage door. Sanj picked up a remote control and pressed a button. The door started to rise and the animals emerged in a neat line.

The vampire kitten next to me mewed a squeaky protest.

"There's nothing you can do now to stop me!" roared Sanj. "So I suppose I can let you out of that booby trap. Release them," he shouted. The blue-footed booby flew over and pulled at the fishing rod, lifting the net off Pradeep, Geeky Girl and Mark. As soon as he was free, Mark raced over and picked up the kitten, but Sanj snatched it back.

"Not so fast. You're a scientist, Mark. I was wondering if we should do an evil experiment? You see, I've hypothesized that the Supersonic Nicifying Helpful Minion Ray won't work on most animals because their instinct supersedes their will."

Mark looked confused. "An animal acts on

instinct, not out of free will," he huffed. "A lion doesn't hunt to be mean; it's acting on instinct!"

"Then why does the ray work on Frankie?" I asked.

"The fish is a zombie. He doesn't have the same instincts as a normal goldfish. He can think for himself. Too bad for him really." Sanj smiled his smarmiest evil smile. "But this kitten is probably the only truly evil animal I've ever seen. I wonder if the ray would work on it?"

"But what if it hurts her?" Mark said, looking worried.

"It might make her less . . . bitey . . . or it might just pop her tiny kitten brain. Let's see, shall we?" Sanj set the vampire kitten on his desk and aimed the sonic ray at her tiny head.

CHAPTER 14

TORTOISE AWAAAAAAAAY!

Geeky Girl covered her eyes and Mark looked too shocked to move. I looked over at Frankie and I swear he winked! Pradeep had clocked it as well. Whatever Frankie was up to, he'd better do it quick.

"Now, Frankie, now!" we both said with our looks.

Just as Sanj was about to set off the ray gun, the blue-footed booby swooped down over his head. It was carrying something.

"Toby!" Pradeep shouted as the tortoise fell from the booby's beak and hurtled toward Sanj.

Sanj looked up and jumped out of the way of

the falling tortoise just in time. Pradeep leaped forward and just managed to catch Toby before he hit the floor, knocking Sanj sideways. But this time Sanj hung onto the ray gun.

The booby made another swoop above our heads.

"What's going on? Stop that bird now, moron fish. Or I'll fry you for dinner!" Sanj yelled as he scrambled to get up.

"That would be terribly high in cholesterol," Geeky Girl whispered through her hands.

Pradeep raced over to Sami with Toby under his arm like a football. I've honestly never seen Pradeep do anything so sporty in my whole life.

The other animals were all out of the garage now and standing on the driveway awaiting orders. All except for Frankie.

Frankie had knocked the glass of water across Sanj's keyboard and was flip-flopping toward Sanj.

"Stop, fish! You are not being nice!" Sanj ordered, and stamped his foot.

"I think Frankie might have been pulling your leg earlier," Pradeep said.

"He doesn't look particularly nice or polite now, does he?" Mark added. "No offense intended, little fishy." Frankie rolled his eyes at Mark and then turned his attention back to Sanj.

"Does this mean you can let the kitten go now?" Mark asked hopefully.

"No! I'm gonna zap that kitten and that moron fish at the same time. Then they'll both do what I say!" Sanj shouted. He aimed the ray gun toward the kitten as she frantically tried to bite her way out of the oven glove.

Then Mark did something that I never expected him to do. He jumped in front of the ray gun! "I'm coming, kitty!" he shouted as he fell. Pradeep, Sami and I covered our ears and Pradeep stamped on the "close" button of the garage-door remote, which had fallen on the floor. Sanj was wearing his ear protectors. But Geeky Girl, Mark, Frankie and the kitten were all exposed. Just as the ray gun went off Mark reached the kitten and cupped his hands over her tiny ears. Geeky Girl grimaced and then fainted on the floor. Mark winced briefly and then fainted as well. Frankie, in his final seconds before passing out, flung himself at Sanj and knocked the ray from his hand. It switched off as it skidded across the floor and knocked into my sneaker. I picked it up.

The room was deathly silent. Frankie twitched on the floor. Pradeep, Sami and I ran over to him. Sami scooped him up and put him in the tank of water but he didn't move. He just floated on the top.

"No swishy fishy," Sami snuffled.

"No matter—I still have my animal army

outside waiting for me," Sanj said, getting up and dusting himself off. "Now that the fish is history, the animals will need someone to give them orders."

Suddenly Frankie's tail swished, his gills fluttered and he opened his eyes and looked up.

"WHOMP! WHOMP! WHOMP!" There was a huge banging sound on the garage door. The sound of lots and lots of pets under Frankie's control. Pets that all held an enormous grudge against Sanj!

"Sanj must have been wrong—Frankie must be immune to the rays after all," Pradeep hissed to me as Sanj backed toward the laundry-room door.

Geeky Girl headed him off. "No way, dude. You're not getting out of here that easily," she said with a scowl.

"Glenda?" Pradeep said.

She glared at him. "What did you call me? Not even my mother calls me by that name anymore!" Her fist clenched into a ball.

"*You* told us! It's a long story," I said. "But you're not nice anymore. I mean, not *really* nice." I couldn't seem to stop myself from digging further into the gaping hole in front of me.

Pradeep saved me. "You're not annoyingly nice anymore," he said, smiling. As he was speaking, Mark stood up and yawned.

"I don't know why I've got a headache, morons, but I know that it's your fault. So I'm gonna pummel you both, and maybe it'll make me feel better."

CHAPTER 15

HAVE YOU HUGGED YOUR VAMPIRE KITTEN TODAY?

Mark raised a fist, but seemed confused that it contained a kitten in an oven glove. "What the . . . ?" he started to say. The kitten looked up at him and mewed, and for a second I thought I saw nice Mark flash across his face. Then he ripped the tape off the oven glove and lifted the kitten out by the scruff of its neck. The kitten looked at him sweetly and then sunk her teeth into his hand.

"Ow! Man, that is one evil cat," Mark yelled, and smiled an Evil Scientist smile.

"Get rid of it," said Sanj. "That ridiculous cat is just distracting you. Go on, pummel them all so we can get out of here and escape from the other pets that are being hypnotically controlled by that stupid zombie goldfish."

"Now I remember," Mark said, putting the kitten into his white coat pocket so that just its head peeked out. "I was gonna splat the fish but you wouldn't let me. And now *you've* got all these zombified pets after *you*"—Mark glared at Sanj— "how is that *my* problem?"

I interrupted. "Um, guys, look up."

As they did, the blue-footed booby swung the fishing rod over their heads and the booby-trap net fell on them! Mark and Sanj looked at each other through the netting.

"Your stupid plans always go wrong," Mark snapped.

"You can't even think up a stupid plan," Sanj spat back. Then the vampire kitten jumped out of Mark's pocket and bit Sanj right on the nose.

"Argh!" yelled Sanj.

"I told you this was one evil cat." Mark said, grinning.

With Mark and Sanj safely booby-trapped, Frankie unzombified all the pets and we put them back in their cages and containers so we could send them back to their homes.

"What should we do with the ray gun?" Pradeep asked.

"We could use it on Mark and Sanj—maybe turn down the setting so they're just a little bit more nice?" I suggested.

Frankie flipped up out of his tank and splashed the gun. The blue-footed booby, still with zombie eyes, waddled over and pecked at it with her beak.

"Zap zap please thank you bad," said Sami solemnly. Frankie had unzombified her now.

"I think Sami is right. We should destroy it so it can't be used on anyone ever again," Pradeep said.

The blue-footed booby flew out of the open garage door with the gun clamped in her beak. She soared way up above the house and then dropped the ray gun so it came crashing down on the driveway.

SMASH! It shattered into a hundred pieces.

"All my hard work ruined," Sanj whined.

We made Sanj pull up the the records of where he got each of the pets and sent e-mails and texts to each owner to let them know their pets were safe and sound and that they could pick them up now. We handed back gerbils, guinea pigs, hamsters, stick insects, lizards, dogs, hamsters,

iguanas and budgies. The owners were all really happy to get them back, even if they were quite confused about how we had managed to find them all. They were still too polite to say anything though.

"I wonder how long it will take for the effects of the ray gun to wear off?" I said when the last kid had left.

"I've looked at Sanj's calculations and at the dosage he gave them, and I think it'll only take a couple of weeks," Pradeep replied.

Just then a van arrived from Bird World to pick up the blue-footed booby and return him to the bird sanctuary, where he was going to be given a new dance floor to practice his tap dancing.

Eventually the only animals left were Geeky Girl's budgie, Boris, Toby the tortoise and the vampire kitten. And Frankie of course!

CHAPTER 16

AN ENEMY IN THE HOUSE

As we stood on Pradeep's driveway watching the
Bird World van drive off, Geeky Girl came up to
Pradeep and me, with Boris the budgie sitting
on her left shoulder like a pirate's parrot that
someone had shot with a shrink ray.

"Um, I just want to say thanks," she said.

Pradeep and I looked at each other. "You're
not turning nice again, are you?" I asked.

Geeky Girl punched my arm.

"Guess not," I added, rubbing my bicep.

"I meant, you know, for saving Boris and
all," she looked down at Pradeep's shoes.
"Man, this being-nice stuff is hard, isn't it."

She smiled and we smiled too.

"Anyway, come around the shop any time. And thanks to your cool fish too," she said, grinning at Frankie, whom I was holding in a glass of water. "He rocks. Just keep him off the net, you know. Just in case anyone's watching." She gave us a knowing smile and turned to walk away.

As she was leaving I swear Boris started hovering just above her shoulder.

Pradeep and I looked at each other. "Naaaahhhh!" we both said.

Just then Mark and Sanj stepped out of the garage holding the shredded remains of the net we had trapped them in. "My kitten has really

sharp teeth," Mark said, balling his fingers into a fist. "So where were we, morons? Oh yeah, I was gonna pummel you."

Frankie's eyes had just started to glow bright green when we heard Pradeep's mom calling from the end of the drive.

"Sanjay!" she yelled. (She always called him that when he was REALLY in trouble.) "Why did the neighbors just ask me if I was opening a pet shop? What have you done to our garage? And why did I get a call from the headmaster at your school to ask if you were allowed out of your room yet? You have a lot of explaining to do, young man . . ." She kept going without even taking a breath.

In one move she scooped Sami onto her hip while her other hand kept up the finger-wagging. Sami waved good-bye as she was carried into the house. "Bye-bye swishy fishy!"

Then we saw my mom's car pull into the driveway next door. Mark had a look on his

face as if he knew he was going to be in for the same earful that Pradeep's mom had just given Sanj. But instead Mom ran over and instantly squealed in that "Oh my gosh that is the cutest thing *ever!*" kind of way that moms do when they see someone else's tiny baby or a cute puppy or kitten.

The vampire kitten was peeking out of Mark's white Evil Scientist coat pocket and had put on its cutest expression for the occasion.

"Where did you come from, you little sweetie?" Mom said in a much higher-pitched voice than normal.

I shot Pradeep a look that said, "Are you sure the bird destroyed the ray gun, because Mom is acting suspiciously nice?"

"Um . . ." Mark got an even-more-confused-than-normal look on his face. "I don't know. I just kinda looked down and it was there."

"Oh, are you a lost little kitty-witty?" Mom cooed at the cat.

"Somebody must own it," I said, and I swear the kitten glared at me.

"Actually, according to Sanj's records, the kitten was returned to the cats' home twenty-seven times for biting. They don't want it back," Pradeep said.

"Oh, you need a home then, don't you, little kitty-witty," Mom said, stroking the kitten behind the ears.

It was just about to sink its teeth into her hand when Mark spotted it opening its mouth and scooped it onto his shoulder.

"Yeah, cos, like, moron over there has the pet fish, so the cat could be my evil sidekick . . . I mean pet," Mark said.

"Well, you'd better bring her inside and we'll get her something to eat and something to drink and a lovely warm place to sleep . . ." Mom was off again. Mark followed her with the vampire kitten perched on his shoulder. He looked back at us and did a quiet "Mwhaa, haaa, haaa,

haaa", and as he did it the kitten made a little "Mewww, meewww, meeww, meew" at the same time.

Frankie jumped up from the glass in my hand when he heard the kitten, and for a moment they glared at each other. The kitten licked her lips, then curled up against Mark's shoulder.

"Hey, Mom, I think the kitten wants fish for dinner," Mark said as he followed Mom into the house.

"Great! Now Mark's not only gone back to being mostly evil but he's got a mostly evil pet too. And one that likes to eat fish," I said.

"I'd get Frankie a lid for his bowl," Pradeep muttered.

Frankie splashed up and nodded in agreement.

"Well, I'd better get Toby back to my cousin's house before he wanders off again," Pradeep said.

"Hey, where *is* Toby?" I asked.

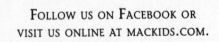